BOOKS

Charlie Hill

Tindal
Street
Press

A complete catalogue record for this book can be obtained from the

The right of Charlie Hill to be identified as the author of
this work has been asserted by him in accordance with the
Copyright, Designs and Patents Act 1988

Copyright © 2013 Charlie Hill

The characters and events in this book are fictitious.
Any similarity to real persons, dead or alive, is coincidental
and not intended by the author.

First published in 2013 by Tindal Street Press,
an imprint of Profile Books Ltd
3A Exmouth House
Pine Street
London ECIR OJH
www.tindalstreet.co.uk

ISBN 978 1 78125 163 8
eISBN 978 1 84765 980 4

Designed and typeset by Tetragon
Printed and bound in Great Britain
by CPI Group (UK) Ltd, Croydon CRO 4YY

10 9 8 7 6 5 4 3 2 1

Charlie Hill is a writer and former bookseller from Birmingham. As well as being the author of *The Space Between Things*, he has written for the *TLS* and the *Independent on Sunday*, and his short stories have appeared in *Ambit*, *Stand* and *The View From Here*.

For Andrea

Acknowledgements

I would like to thank, in no particular order: Rachael McKee, Clare McClure, Tony Roberts, Luke Brown, Alan Mahar, Andy Killeen, Becky from Stourbridge, Lisa Hoftizer, Nick James, Mum and Dad, and Hannah and Drew.

BOOKS

Introducing a bookselling anti-hero

It was three o'clock on Saturday afternoon, the end of a typically long week, and Richard Anger – the owner of the last little bookshop in town – was waiting for a cab to take him to the airport.

He held a small rucksack. In it, a pair of shorts, a shirt, two pairs of pants, a pair of flip-flops and a beach read. The book was by David Foster Wallace. Richard had put his favourite 'Gone Readin'' sign in the window of the shop and he hoped that this would be the case: he'd started the bloody thing half a dozen times and had yet to get beyond the first ten pages.

Despite the promise of four days of sun and overly sweet wine, Richard was sporting a sour puss. But then that was to be expected – he sold books for a living, after all. During the course of an average year, he could reasonably expect to afford a weekend away at the seaside; that he always flew somewhere warm was due in part to an original take on debt management and in part to the need for relief from the uniquely draining nature of his day job.

Richard was pushing forty and had run Back Street Books for nearly a decade and a half. He'd started it up as an outlet for his passion for books, a passion that had only dissipated with the appropriation of the phrase 'A Passion for Books' by 'The Nation's Favourite

Bookseller'. Back Street Books was a genuine labour of bloody-minded love, its shelves demonstrating the most minor of concessions to mainstream taste. It specialised instead in anything that Richard liked to read: long-forgotten noir fiction, modernist classics, chapbooks, transgressive experimentation, translated erotica, minimalism, short stories, satires, samizdat, surrealist poetry and smut.

Initially this indulgence paid off. For the first few years of the operation, the pages of his balance sheet turned serenely enough. But then Richard had planted in fertile ground. Despite its name, the shop was actually situated on the High Street of Harborne, a suburb of south Birmingham, and Harborne was a genuine reader's suburb. Half a mile in one direction and you'd find people who felt politically obliged to take their Julian Barnes with a James Kelman; half a mile in the other and people looking for the latest Lee Child could be persuaded – with only a modicum of bullshit – to leave with a Patricia Highsmith.

Even so, Back Street Books was lucky to have survived for so long. There had been another independent on the high street when Richard had opened up and a Christian bookshop too. The former had succumbed to the usual: commercial pressures, decreasing literacy rates, the rise of the machines, yada yada. And if – as Richard liked to think – the demise of the latter was down to his determined championing of Dawkins, Hitchens et al., there was no getting away from the fact that, whichever way you cut it, it was a bad time to be in bookselling.

It was getting worse too. Business was epochmakingly slow. The figures at the end of this year's first quarter had been the most harrowing thing Richard had read since the last Ben Elton. Indeed, it was only due to luck that Richard had scraped together the necessary for four days on the Med. Two months ago he'd invested £25 in a dead-cert internet betting scam that involved covering your losses with amateur bookmakers in the Irish Republic. While he was keeping personal tabs on one of his runners at Ripon racecourse, the rain which went on to wash out the meeting caused a flash flood that picked up his Skoda Felicia and swept it away down the River Skell. By the time a farmer and his wife had fished it out of a hedge some way down the A61, the car was a write-off and Richard only had to sit back, wait for the insurance and plan his trip to Corfu.

And yet. Even now, with his flight just two hours away, he was struggling to get enthused. What was concerning him was how long he could carry on like this. Was this his last year as the owner of a bookshop? As his own man? How long would it be before he was arrested on the pavement outside a boarded-up shop, drunk and naked, hurling books and abuse at the slow-moving traffic and its indifferent cargo?

A day and a half later, waking in a hotel room, slouching upright and gasping for air, Richard was past caring. All night he had been sweating wine, and his sheets were damp and sweet and sour. He waved away an imaginary mosquito, reached over to his bedside table, felt for his soft-pack cigarettes. He lit one, then exhaled in surprise, offended by the taste in his mouth. Then he coughed, a phlegm-filled hack that burnt his lungs.

The holiday was clearly doing its job. Richard hadn't thought about merchandising or profit and loss or refunds ('This book is supposed to be funny. It isn't. I want my money back') for over twenty-four hours. And despite the fact that he was sure he was about to have a stroke, he felt quantifiably better than he had in Blighty. He shuffled to the bathroom mirror and gave himself a celebratory scowl. It was a practised expression and Richard was happy that it was the expression of a truly bad man...

He tried hard to be bad, did Richard. Playing the anti-hero was his reason to be. Not that it had always been the case. Just over a dozen short years ago he'd been ensconced in a respectable suburb, engaged to be married and a long way removed from thoughts of bad behaviour. His attitude had changed only when his fiancée Julie contrived to have an affair. It was a very off-the-shelf number – literally so; she had met the fella in the 'Exotic Ideas' aisle of the local Tesco – and at first Richard hadn't given it long. The two of them were clearly not suited. When he saw them on the street together and they smiled at him, everything between them seemed so lifeless and polite. There was no sign whatever of the extravagant rows which he and Julie had enjoyed. And without any feelings of rancour or bitterness, how could they hope to experience true passion?

But Richard might have been wrong. Julie and her new man had gone on to get married just six months later. Six poxy months. This betrayal had left him heartbroken and furious and – in terms of the remainder of what promised to be a sad and angry life – in need of a plan. Fortunately, this was not long in presenting itself.

The most galling thing about the affair, he decided, was the obviousness of it all. The sheer mundanity of his lover's disloyalty. Julie might have thought that she was dallying in forbidden pleasures, but she wasn't. The man's name was Jeff, for God's sake. A Sven or a Luigi he could have lived with, but Jeff? They had met in Tesco's. Not at a poker school or a cockfight, but at a supermarket. And the brand-leading supermarket at that. Furthermore, when Richard had asked her 'why?' all that she had said was that he 'didn't pay her enough attention'. I mean. Please. Nothing there about Jeff's devotion to the Ancient Order of Shaolin Monks or his passion for parascending or S&M. Nothing, in fact, of any lasting significance whatsoever. No, the two of them were autopiloting in mute acquiescence through the prescribed pleasures of the echt-suburban gloop. Middle of the road didn't cover it – it was utterly, miserably and unforgivably mediocre.

From that moment on Richard had been the sworn enemy of mediocrity in all its manifestations. If that was all that Julie wanted from life, well, she was welcome to it. Welcome to her mediocre lover and their passionless affair, the unexceptional children they'd doubtless spawn and the plank-like camber-averse friends who'd come to call with their unoriginal take on their unoriginal world. Richard would show her that he was better than that. He would be different.

There'd be no such humdrummity for him.

The way forward was not difficult to pin down. Mediocrity was out. Goodness was way beyond his ken. And that, he was delighted to see, left bad behaviour.

But how best to be bad? The fundamentals seemed simple enough. There'd be lots of drinking and drug-taking and painstakingly casual efforts to bed as many women as possible. Other stuff would doubtless present itself as well, for Richard was sure that badness led to badness and more of the same.

He threw himself into his role. He found himself a natural when it came to the sauce – this part of his plan was a piece of piss. He liked liquor. You knew where you were with the stuff. It was a constant, reliable presence, always there, waiting just around the corner, to lift you, take you up and off and away. And so he returned to a number of inner-city pubs he'd frequented in his time with Julie. He left them in the early morning. He drank on his own at home and he drank from cans while walking down the street. He found himself mullered, mashed and soured, swallied-up and unwell. And then, inexorably, and with the help of more of the same, he found himself better again.

Richard took drugs as well: weed and E and billy and what he was told was cocaine. The weed he found frustrating – he wasn't one for introversion – even if the E was diverting enough and the stimulants fun. But he was disappointed to discover that such behaviour wasn't far enough removed from the everyday to be anything *but* mediocre. Any of the pubs towards town – or at least those that displayed a 'Drug Dealers Will be Prosecuted' sign – were a cert for hash, and chemicals could always be found among the older generation of well-heeled bohos in the suburb of Moseley Village, where he sometimes passed a Sunday lunchtime. It all seemed like too little trouble to be worth it.

Then there were the women. The women hadn't proved too much of an ask either. Most of them had admittedly been on some kind of convoluted search for marbles but then Richard wasn't consulting them about investment portfolios or the roadblocks to peace in the Middle East. During the first summer of his new resolve, he had met with alarming success and trailed bad sex like a slug. There'd been a lass who worked behind the bar of his local, then her sister and then, somewhat belatedly, her daughter, who had a thing for prescription chemicals and an unnecessary glint in her eye. All had helped him over the hump.

Only once did he have cause to question his cavalier attitude to the opposite sex. Richard would often end his Saturday night session in Selly Oak. The suburb was home to the university but there were attractions for a man of his proclivities too: the streets were covered in litter and rats and there were pubs and kebab shops and dark alleys full of launderette steam and undergrad piss that held the promise of nefarious goings-on.

One of these led to the offices of Richard's traditional end-of-night taxi stop. The door next to the taxi firm's belonged to the business above: the Pussy Palace Sauna and Grill. It announced its presence with a pink neon sign that flickered on to the side street and it looked as salubrious as it sounded. One night, worn out after a heroic four-hour after-work sup and faced with an unusually long wait for a cab, Richard decided to take an exploratory mooch. Whether this was prompted by a genuine desire to test the boundaries of bad behaviour in the manner of a Bukowski-esque spit-and-sawdust anti-hero, or merely by pissed-up curiosity, Richard wasn't sure.

He rang the bell of the Pussy Palace and walked up a damp and narrow staircase. Through another door there was a desk where a woman, or girl, was sitting. She was dolled-up, and the description can never have been more apt: her eyes were bright yet unsmiling and her smile was unsmiling too. As Richard approached the desk, she put down the book she was reading – he was surprised to see that it was *Crime and Punishment* – and said, 'Hello, I'm Nikki.'

Even in his befuddled state Richard wondered whether that was her actual name. Not that he hung around to find out. Wherever it had come from, his curiosity had been summarily satisfied. The Pussy Palace was a dismal place. And there was something about Nikki that made it impossible for him to square his contrarian take on the sex industry with the fact that it was a bit too close to the grubby side of bad behaviour for comfort.

Still, this misjudgement aside, things were going well. If not exactly bad, his behaviour was a long way removed from that which would be considered acceptable by Julie and her new 'boyfriend'. There was just one problem. Behaving badly for the sake of it – or even as part of some pissant personal vendetta – was such a cliché it was mediocre in itself. Worse, if his every transgression was directed solely at his ex-lover, then she had surely won their little psycho-sexual tussle. Richard needed more. Something that would place his antipathy to mediocrity in a wider context. He needed a sense of purpose.

As always he had looked to writing to help him. Richard fancied himself as a writer. Not of novels, not just yet, not while there was still living to be done. But putting words on a page helped him to better indulge his passions. It gave them substance, convinced him that his whims and behaviours had a gravitas, however rabid that gravitas was. And so he scribbled, high on cocaine, furiously and without compromise, snarling away about dirty-bombs and bending before The Man. He doodled experimentally, stoned, about suits and ties and uniforms and public nudity and Gilbert and George and the sausages you find in greasy-spoon breakfasts and organic eggs over-easy or with hominy grits and the secret lives of people who drove the buses...

It was to no avail.

It was on a bus on a Sunday evening that Richard found his sense of purpose. He was sitting at the back, singing songs with an ageing dipso he'd met in a pub that lunchtime. The man had three fingers on one hand and wore shades when he played pool. When the singing started, a few of the other passengers moved down the bus, looking back nervously at the raucous miscreants. They huddled together, animated. They muttered and shook their heads, unaware, perhaps, that Richard and his new best pal were actually singing a medley of hits by the Carpenters.

Richard saw the effect of his behaviour and he was happy. There was nothing pissant about what he was doing, after all. By behaving badly he was causing consternation, stimulating debate. He was provoking people – and he was sure that this wasn't reading too much into the situation – into questioning the way they saw the world. Being bad was a moral responsibility. Without people breaking the rules – without people like him – how would morality evolve? It was all very well the Jeffs or Julies of this world indulging in their oh-so-snooze-worthy workaday affairs, but humankind needed the bad to work out how best to live. This was why he needed to misbehave. This was his purpose. To provoke. *To be a provocateur...*

In his hotel room, Richard showered with just the right amount of conviction. The trip had begun promisingly but now it was time to up the pace. He draped himself in his finest Hunter Thompson shirt and headed for the bar.

Introducing the writing of a heroine, relaxing on holiday

By seven in the morning the low-slung ceiling fan was already struggling to stir the air in her room. Mindful as she was of her resolution to have a good trip, conditions were undoubtedly trying.

She had come to the town after three days at Perivoli, a small village on the southern coast where she had heard the photography was exceptional. It had proved disappointing.

The scenery had been stunning, the flora dense and varied. Dusty dirt tracks led away from the road by the sea past clutches of crocus and anemone, striped red and purple and white. Higher up, the paths turned rocky and wound through thick bougainvillea, ground-hugging clouds of deep pink, magenta and cerise, heavy with pollen. Every so often the brilliant yellow flowers of Spanish broom blazed like flares or shone through, misty like the sun. Eucalyptus trees, their trunks wind-sculpted, their bark in strips of russet and green, lent the landscape a sense of perspective; from certain points, the hills offered views of a turquoise and tranquil sea that was rounded and immense and hinting at depths that were less benign.

There was much else that teased and pulled at the senses. The sweet perfume of what she guessed was wild rosemary and myrtle, the sharpness of oregano and medicinal density of sage. She had seen goats and lizards. Birds called on the wing, dipping and disappearing in the haze. The air was cooler here than at sea level but there was little shade and the paths were more uneven, making progress slow.

Once, on a walk up the side of a hill that had become a little more taxing than she had anticipated, she had reached a small plateau where she'd found the remains of a building. She sat on a low wall until her breathing had slowed and then she began to explore. The ruins intrigued her. It was an old sheep farmer's cottage perhaps, or an elaborate shelter for his charges. Whatever its purpose, it seemed to have emerged from the hillside itself, its walls thick like boulders, the skeleton of its roof bound in tendrils of ivy-like vines that stemmed thickly from the earth. She picked her way carefully into the building's shade. It was ripe in there. She thought she smelled honeysuckle and was momentarily distracted. Then a flutter of birds flew out of the corner of her eye and past her into the sunlight and she was startled and thrilled. Goldfinches! She hadn't expected to see them this far into the hills...

On that particular occasion she had shot nearly a whole roll of film. And it wasn't until she was back at her guest house, waiting for a plate of evening *mezedes*, that she began to feel the first distant aches of dissatisfaction with her efforts on the trip to date. She was happy that the pictures she had were distinctive enough in their own way – each day she had ventured slightly farther inland and had been careful to capture the subtle changes in flora that had resulted from her extra effort – but compositionally they had one thing in common: something was missing.

It was people. She hadn't expected to see anyone, of course; she hadn't met a soul on any of her previous walks and if she thought she might this time, she might not have bothered making the trip. But despite her desire for solitude, she found herself craving the sight of people.

There was an order to photography. A way of doing things, a sequence that required of the photographer a particular engagement with the world. For her, taking a picture meant that the most chaotically inspired, the most emotionally charged moment needed to be – however briefly – viewed dispassionately. There was something about this process that she found deeply satisfying. Necessary even. She had experienced this satisfaction on a few occasions on the trip; photographing an unruly tangle of flowers that needed arranging, an insect that needed framing just so. But if you put people in the picture, well, the stakes were raised, the satisfaction became more than merely a matter of aesthetics. Because people could be contained, preserved, *kept in their place* through their exposure to this process. At the click of a button.

On the morning of her second day in Corfu Town, she left her hotel after a light breakfast and wandered around photographing people. She captured them arguing in front of the ochre cafés of the Spinanda, enjoying respite from the sun in the many churches or themselves photographing the Georgian terraces of the Liston. At two in the afternoon, she returned to her room and took a shower. By now she was looking forward to venturing out in the early evening, to record the people of the town at play.

She walked into the taverna at about four in the afternoon. She was wearing a simple white sunhat, a pale yellow cotton dress and a pair of faded leather sandals. She ordered a slightly sparkling mineral water at the bar and asked about food and then she made her way to a table.

Richard was already half in the bag. He had looked up from his glass of wine as this poppet, no, maybe not, this num-nums, no, that wasn't right, *get a grip, man*, this *vision* had entered. Now he stared at her, in awe. A stomach-sinking feeling of desperation washed over him, the sort that he'd felt many times when five grand had gone tits-up at the last ditch of the last race. This time it came from somewhere else, from a beauty that Richard couldn't begin to explain or hope to possess. The woman was slightly off-centre, funny looking, even. She moved like a breeze. Her voice was a sponge on a fevered brow. She had a coolness about her and at that moment Richard wanted nothing more than to bask in her cool.

Lauren Furrows sat at a table in the middle of the taverna. It was a small place and quite busy but quiet enough for her to relax and consider her options for the afternoon. For a moment she was distracted by the light in the room. It was good – clear and muted – and she wondered whether she should ask if she could take some photographs. But no. First she would have a drink and a bite to eat.

She watched as the hands of a clock moved unhurriedly on a wall. The clientele was mixed. Near the door, a man and woman in their thirties sat at a table. They were each reading, he a fat, garishly covered book with a title in English, she a loosely bound A4 manuscript. A young local couple – Lauren had them down as friends of the owner – sat close together at the bar and talked in coded love. The bartender was exchanging cigarette smoke with another local, an old man with his face wrapped around his head like bark around a tree. The man on the table next to her was...

Lauren started. My word. What *was* he doing? Well, staring, obviously. In what looked like dumb fascination. Now he was... my God, what was that? Was he trying to communicate something? Yes, yes he was. He was trying to smile. It was a little lopsided maybe, but that was what it was. What a strange – and unquestionably drunk – man. And what a hideous shirt!

Ignoring him, she looked away, sipped from her glass of water and rubbed the back of her neck with her hand. She was still not used to the humidity of the island. Reaching for her camera, she flicked a few switches, set it down on the table and waited. After five minutes, the local couple left the taverna. There was little noise. The clock made no sound. The bartender was writing out a menu on a chalkboard. The old man was sucking a coffee. Lauren flexed her fingers, picked up her camera again. She liked the feel of the bar, the way that the personalities of the people there were indivisible from the environment, held in place by stone, captured by the surfaces of the ceramic tiles behind the bar. She could do something striking if she picked the right time, she was sure of that. As she had with the cyclist in the quad that evening last summer when the light was pink and the sky was strawberry rippled. She'd waited until he'd got off and was chaining his bike up before she'd taken the picture. And the two lovers she'd spied lying on the grass in the park, she'd watched them for a while, until she'd started to feel uncomfortable with their closeness. Portraiture was all a matter of timing. There was no rush. She decided she would order something to eat. She looked to the table next to her to check on the state of her neighbourly drunk.

At the next table, Richard was slowly emerging from his state of shock. The wine was taking short cuts around his brain and his hapless desire had been replaced with a frenzied need. He *had* to have her, this woman who could never be his, he simply *had* to have her. But how best to approach her? Richard was aware that his extreme behaviour was not to everyone's taste. He would have to approach from downwind for a start...

After what seemed like a terrible age of anticipation, Richard settled on spillage. It was something of a cliché maybe, but it would give him the opportunity to demonstrate both his contrarian take on good manners – despite himself he liked them – and his practised approach to the removal of potentially embarrassing stains.

There were only a couple of flaws in the plan. First, he wasn't in spilling distance. Secondly, the woman was not sitting on any route that he could realistically take to the bar. Spillage seemed a less plausible scenario than splashage and given the distance between the two of them even that would mean the wine would have to travel a distance of well over six feet. Richard was not sure that he could pass this off as an accident. And the line between a little bit of badness and violently hoying a bottle of wine across a quiet taverna was a thin one.

Just as Richard was contemplating feigning a seizure of some kind, the woman who sat reading at the table next to the door dropped her reading matter, pirouetted off her seat and pitched face first on to the stone floor. The woman's companion caught his breath sharply and was calling her name even as Lauren was crossing the bar towards the prostrate figure with a controlled purpose that tugged at Richard's loins.

When Richard saw the writer's name on the cover of the manuscript the woman had been reading, slick as a lech, he saw his chance to make an impression.

'I'm not surprised she's nodded off,' he said, 'reading that rubbish.'

SNAPS

Lauren Furrows sat in a pale green room and sipped a cup of peppermint tea. She worked on the campus of the University of Birmingham, in a handsome brick-red Edwardian building of the Byzanto-Italian school. Her office overlooked a quadrangle of grass that was enclosed by small-windowed and immaculately weathered Victorian blocks. A sycamore stood serenely in the centre of the square. Chittering martins and skittish swifts holidayed in the eaves above her window while down below learners and lovers gathered and sprawled and read or were read to by others.

On the worst of days, the view was diverting. Today, however, the early September sky was blue, the sun shone, the birds sang and yet still Lauren was not to be diverted. All morning she had been conscious of a question darting swift-like around her brain and she had spent at least half of this time on the phone, attempting to relieve herself of the burden of her concern. It hadn't helped.

The cause of her fixation was a newsfeed in the online journal *Neurology Today*. It was only a few lines long but its significance outweighed its brevity:

Two deaths this summer have been attributed to a previously unknown condition dubbed Spontaneous Neural Atrophy Syndrome, or SNAPS. The first victim was a British holidaymaker who died suddenly on the island of Corfu. The condition came to light following a joint investigation between the British consul, the Greek police and medical authorities in the area, and the syndrome went on to claim the life of the British consul himself.

Examinations undertaken by a local coroner and Sofia Georgiou, a neuro-specialist from the mainland, suggest that the condition is characterised by a spontaneous weakening and failure of the electrical signals that pass through the cells of the brain. Its cause is not known but its pathology – a precipitous cortical degradation – is thought to be similar to that identified as Sudden Onset Cerebrovascular Trauma in a journal article by Lauren Furrows in 2009 (*Furrows, L (2009) Qualitative Neurological Research*).

Now Lauren was gratified to be referenced in a journal as auspicious as *Neurology Today*. But this particular peer acknowledgement came with caveats.

The article was sloppy, with insufficient attention to detail. It contained assertions that lacked even the most rudimentary of empirical underpinning. Lauren's career had been dedicated to the investigation of conditions such as 'SNAPS', and if there was one thing that she could reasonably assert, it was that axons didn't spontaneously weaken and fail without reason. What external factors had triggered the cortical failure? And why didn't this aspect of the syndrome's pathology merit a mention?

Lauren had worked too hard to allow her reputation to be compromised by association with a piece as amateurish as this. So. She would get to the bottom of this SNAPS business. And in a quietly satisfying rebuke to the careless tone of the newsfeed, she would do so methodically, incrementally and without recourse to unsubstantiated conjecture.

She began her investigations after lunch. The first phone call she made was to the editor of *Neurology Today*. She discovered that the piece had been put together by an intern, from a news agency report. The reference to her work had come from the editor himself who was familiar with Lauren's research in the field. Her next call was to the news agency and then, after five minutes, to the British consul in Patras; later in the afternoon there followed a brief exchange of emails with all parties, some of which she cross-referenced.

Over the course of these communications, Lauren gleaned much. The Greek coroner was conversant with the common causes of brain death and had demonstrated the necessary methodology in ruling them out. But still the questions remained. What *had* caused the deaths? Were they even connected? And – if it existed – just what was SNAPS?

There were elements of this story that Lauren was struggling with. It was clear that if she was to understand the issues that the identification of this new syndrome had raised, she would have to broaden her observations.

Lauren made another cup of tea, thought of her alternatives. She thought back to the death she had witnessed. There had been other people in the taverna, other tourists. They might have noticed something that she had missed. Someone in particular came to mind, someone she'd spoken to at some length in the aftermath of the incident, someone who had been pleased to discover that they lived in the same city. What had he said he did? 'I run the last bookshop in town.' It wouldn't be too difficult to track him down, then.

Independent bookselling

Richard Anger opened up late that morning. This was not the existential ball-ache he imagined it must be for his fellow shopkeepers. It was of little consequence to his daily routine – he was often late – and it did not adversely affect his mood: Richard had no desire to live in a society where the buses ran on time, still less to pander to the whims of shoppers who wanted to buy anything at one minute past nine in the morning.

On this particular occasion he'd spent the previous night on an extended mooch around the Irish quarter of Birmingham. The session had kicked off with a few port and Guinnesses and then – inspired by a sudden burst of bleary Europhilia – he'd switched to Trappist-brewed fruit beer. The combination had been effective in settling the nerves but, despite this, it hadn't been the most successful of his forays into the Digbeth netherworld.

Richard was drunk by the time he'd clocked his night hadn't had the necessary karmic imprimatur of truly bad behaviour. If he hadn't been, he might not have approached a man whose face he recognised from that year's surprise summer bestseller, a photographic celebration of 'The Hard Men of Brum'. At first the fella in question had been civil enough. But when Richard's attempts to ingratiate himself led him to assume the persona of a self-confessed 'tasty geezer', the sociopath's tolerance had begun to pall. At around two in the morning he'd beckoned Richard close and muttered something in his ear. Richard thought he must have misheard. When he realised he hadn't, he decided to leave the pub, the better to preserve his dignity and what he guessed were his kneecaps.

Since then he'd managed to piece together only six fractured hours of sleep. And he was suffering. Not that he had a hangover, mind. Richard didn't do hangovers. For him headaches, the fear of loud noises and the like were the stuff of caricature. Instead, he felt ill. Seriously, anxiously unwell. He was jittery and tense and felt faint. His fingers and toes were numb. His vision was blurred. A toxic foreboding trickled down the channels in his brain.

The state of his shop didn't help. The last thing before he'd left the previous evening, he'd had to contend with a sudden rush of schoolchildren. They'd missed the bus, noticed one of Richard's more eye-catching window displays – the transcript of an imagined conversation between D.H. Lawrence, Anaïs Nin, Michel Houellebecq and Erica Jong – and decided to familiarise themselves with the oeuvres in question. In itself, this was manageable, but a tricky situation arose when, their appetite for the printed word whetted, they'd reached the coffee-table Mapplethorpes. Were they sixteen? They certainly weren't eighteen. Should Richard score one for the libertines and let them have a look? It was not an abstract dilemma and, reluctant to go to prison for a cause as morally nebulous as this, he threw them out. (As much as Richard liked the idea of an urban underclass of disaffected and rebellious youth, he didn't want them in his shop.) This led to another trashed display and the loss of a sale to the nervous-looking youth with the pink drainpipe jeans who had been waiting to talk to Richard about – he guessed – Banana Yoshimoto.

Richard made himself a coffee, reshaped the paper-backs in the window into a display which, despite his best efforts, remained stubbornly un-penis-like. He switched on the till and perused the morning's post. As usual, it was full of books. There was something dulling about this ritual. Many publishers had stopped using sales reps and pitched to retailers by sending through new titles in the post instead. And every day, Richard despaired at the mediocrity of the new arrivals. The difficulty was that mediocrity took many forms. There was mediocre/good, mediocre/bad, mediocre/indifferent – the stuff was everywhere. He did what he could to satisfy his conscience, to ignore the sort of writing that he felt was merely words on paper, a smooth progression from point A to point B that detracted from the sum total of the human experience. But deep down, Richard suspected he was pissing into the wind.

Today, he'd been sent three memoirs and three attempts at fiction. *A Long Way from Under the Mango Tree,* a tale of inter-generational conflict from inside the Anglo-Pakistani community, lumped its exotic bulk ahead of *Learning to Walk* – from seventeen-year-old diva Lil' Missy Muffet – and *Boom! (Bang-a-Bang),* an inside story of the financial crisis written by a deeply penitent millionaire; *Sophie's Party Time* by Trixi Hart, *Commander Down!* by Johnny 'Two Splints' Morrison and *My Mates*, a 'grittily realistic' collection of short stories from the backstreets of Burton upon Trent, completed the line-up.

Richard shook his head. It was more of the same old same old, a steady accretion of grim. Where were the dazzlers, the men and women on the edge of their art, those who would present the world not as it sometimes seemed – muddy, impressionistic, torporific – but as it should be – brilliant and intriguing, perverse and beautiful and vile? Those who would rent and tear at the fabric of mediocrity? Those who would move us on?

He yawned loudly, scratched his armpit and juggled his balls in an attempt to take his mind off his alarmingly tocking ticker. His phone rang and he picked it up. Then he heard the voice on the other end and found himself in the middle of his third hot flush of the morning.

Blimey!

'Hello,' said the voice. 'This is Lauren, Lauren Furrows. Is this Richard Anger?'

'It certainly is,' said Richard. His heart thumped an offbeat. Sweating mightily, he sat back on his stool and swung his feet on to the counter in a gesture designed to affirm – to himself at least – his ability to nonchalantly absorb the shocking reappearance of his holiday infatuation. 'Bollocks!' he spat, as his grittily realistic coffee went flying.

The voice continued.

'We met in Corfu. Do you remember?'

Shit a brick did Richard remember.

'Oh yes. The photographer?' he asked, tossing a coffee-soaked Waxy: the Cultural History of the Wax Crayon into the bin.

'Photography is just a hobby. I'm a Professor of Neurology at the university.'

'I see. What can I do you for?'

'I'll get straight to the point. I need to ask you some questions about that afternoon.'

'Blimey. Well, fire away. I'm all yours.'

'I was rather hoping we could meet up,' said Lauren, 'if that's OK? The situation is a little sensitive, you see.'

A bad afternoon

The promise of that evening's meeting with Lauren twisted away from the jittery Richard all day. Just what did the woman want? Richard had fun speculating. Maybe she was going to tell him she'd spent the last few months struggling to grasp the depth of her feelings for him, or that she wanted to become a silent partner in Back Street Books. Such absurdity was a welcome diversion. Because from the moment his conversation with Lauren had ended, Richard's day had otherwise been one long reminder of his ongoing unsuitability for the title of World's Most Joyous Man.

That morning he'd shifted a total of six books. He'd had to rebuff – politely and then not so – two self-published fantasists looking for a face-out on his precious shelves. And then he'd been exposed to an ethical question, his second in a day.

It was an obvious dilemma, though no less intractable for that. A woman – not one of his 'regulars' – had approached him with an enquiry: 'My boyfriend's really into serial killers. What would you recommend?' Richard knew what she was after. He'd seen the like, in Waterstones and discount bookstores. Badly written paperbacks packed with official police photographs that recorded in unnecessarily voyeuristic detail scarcely conceivable acts of violence. Porn, in other words, and not the excusable stuff either. Richard had laid a funny on the woman – 'I'd start by getting myself

27

a new boyfriend if I were you' – before selling her a copy of *The Executioner's Song*. Richard loved the book and there was a chance that the woman and her proto-dicer would too. But it was a slim one. More to the point, who was he to try to influence their reading habits? The whole thing smacked of paternalism. If people wanted to read shit, shouldn't bookshops just sell them shit to read?

On this occasion, Richard was in no mood to address the subtleties of the question. Rather than try – and emboldened by a lunchtime dip into Lester Bangs – he'd decided to perk up his afternoon by writing a blog post.

Richard's blog was called The Bilious Bibliophile. It was infrequently updated. Its tag line was 'Informed, irreverent and arsey'; 'Ill-judged, embittered and half-hearted' would have been closer to the mark. He was working on a posting about the future of the book and the way that this was intimately bound up in the cultural jizz-fest that surrounded electronic publishing.

The previous year had seen Richard numbed daily by the drip drip drip of industry-wide equivocation about the latest technological developments in the biz. Panic had greeted the news that e-books had started to outsell hardback fiction. The book as ink on paper, a spine, the cover, looked finished. On the flipside, some were arguing that the torrent of downloadable lulus and vanity-published genre stuff and Kindle-friendly niche stuff would reinvigorate the word. Democratise the language, transform the industry. Some said the book itself as object of desire wouldn't be missed:

the future was simply about the most effective way for text to reach the reader. These were fascinating questions, questions that interrogated the bullshit spread by industry analysts, even as they provided them with more to spread.

In the last month, determined to ignore the speculations of others in favour of his own, Richard had begun to size up the competition. He read the top-selling self-published Kindle titles, those hawked by the market-leading Print on Demand outfits, the best of the subsidy presses. And notwithstanding the odd decent chapbook publisher, he'd discovered that all the innovations had actually delivered was a flood of fucking awful writing.

The book looked doomed, assailed on all sides by those who'd see it superseded by the synthetic-new and those who didn't give two shiny ones. With the recession forging ahead with renewed vigour, bookselling too was going the way of papyrus, taking with it what was left of Richard's self-esteem, his beer money and his comedic persona.

It was nearly enough to make you give up, on books and what they meant to people and on the book itself...

Richard witnesses the theft of a book

Antsy and glum, Richard left work and headed to the pub. He had a couple of hours to kill before he met up with Lauren and had decided to sharpen his wits with a couple of pints of real ale. On the way he popped into Sainsbury's. They were doing a sluiceable drop of house red in a plastic bottle – it came out at £2.34 a litre – and he wanted to lay some down.

Richard was leaving the supermarket when he saw Muzz, a beggar. He'd known him for about a month. They'd met when Muzz had asked Richard for some change outside the shop and Richard had noticed a battered copy of *The Lord of the Rings* sticking out of his coat pocket. They'd started talking. Muzz slept on floors and in doorways on the street. Richard couldn't be sure he was on hard drugs but the signs were there; every time he saw him he'd be clutching a tin of milk-based health drink.

On this occasion, Muzz was by the stands of books and magazines, looking as nonchalant as it is possible for a tramp to look. As Richard watched he reached up, grabbed a fat Tom Clancy from the top shelf, slipped it into his bag and was out of the doors, down the steps and away. Richard was shocked. He didn't need this, not today. It was the broadest of daylight. Anyone might have seen. He hurried after his acquaintance, gobbets of indignation at the ready.

'What the hell do you think you're doing?' he said.

'Oh. Hello, Richard,' said Muzz. 'You saw that, did you? I can explain...'

'You'd better. You're lucky I don't drop you in it. What the hell do you think you're doing? I thought you said you were over all that now?'

'I am. I am. Honest I am.'

'So what the hell was that, then?'

'Look, it's not what you think. I can explain.'

'Go on then. And this had better be good.'

'It's like this. The security guard in Waterstones in the city centre, he clocks me every time I go in. I can't hardly move without him following me. But they've got this thing where they don't mind doing exchanges. You know, providing the book's in good nick they'll swap it, even without a receipt. So I go to Sainsbury's, help myself, get it to Waterstones and upgrade. So far I've managed to swap Jeffrey Archer for Glenn Duncan, a Louise Bagshawe for a Beryl Bainbridge and *Breaking Dawn* for *The Blind Assassin*.'

'*Breaking Dawn?*'

'Twilight: Book 4.'

'Really?' said Richard. 'Well. OK, then. But only if you're sure. I don't want to see you getting back into your bad old ways. What's next?'

'Think I'm going to go for those short stories you mentioned. You know, by that dead woman...'

'Ah. The Katherine Mansfield. OK, then. Just so's you do...'

'I will. See you, Richard.'

'See you, Muzz.'

Holding it together

Richard met Lauren that evening in a busy pub just off campus. He'd suggested the place with his delicate state in mind: he knew that keeping Lauren off balance would help him to maintain what passed for his equilibrium.

He'd used the place about five years ago, but it wasn't how he remembered it. He hadn't expected a Toby Carvery – that was the whole point – but he couldn't help thinking he'd overplayed his hand somewhat. The bar was done out in bright yellow. The bar staff had name badges. There were promotions on blue and green bottled drinks. The music thumped. It was full of students drinking, being silly and loud, all glassy-eyed wonder, white teeth and flashes of tit. Richard resented their uncomplicated drunken rowdiness – young people, what did they know about bad behaviour? – and then felt queasy at his resentment.

He ordered a brandy and pep and propped up the bar. Since leaving work he'd indulged his despondency; now he was in a satisfactorily foul mood. This was familiar ground and it could only help in his efforts to keep himself together during his encounter with his mystery woman.

Lauren walked into the pub. She stopped for a moment just inside the door and Richard caught his breath. Ever since she'd called, he'd been piecing together what few details he remembered of her from

Corfu. The result had been tantalising enough but it was nothing like the woman in the flesh. Lauren ordered a lime and soda and they sat down at the only place that was free, next to a table of hockey players playing a drinking game called – by all accounts – Fuzzy Duck.

'And so,' said Richard, 'we meet again.'

'*I'm sorry?*'

'*We meet again.*'

To his right someone dropped a glass. Someone else started singing. The bass thudded. Lauren looked around and shook her head.

'Why did you suggest we come here?' she said.

'*What?*'

'*Why did we come here? It's not very appropriate.*'

'*I don't know really. I suppose I thought it would be convenient.*'

'*Thank you. I think.*'

'*I mean, don't get me wrong. It's not my type of place. I mean, I think it's full of...*'

Richard dismissed the bar staff, the drinks promotions and the principle of universal access to education with a wave of his hand, and stumbled for the right phrase. Behind him two girls argued over what tune to play next as the music stopped abruptly.

'*... arseholes,*' said Richard.

Lauren frowned. The music started up again and she moved her chair round to Richard's side of the table.

'That's a charming sentiment. I did tell you I'm a professor at this university? Yes? Well then. Do you mind if we get down to business? I really don't want to spend any more time in here than I have to.'

'You're the boss,' said Richard.

Lauren frowned.

'So. Anyway. I take it you remember the woman who died in the taverna on Corfu?'

She told him then about SNAPS and complained about the implications of people associating her name with the syndrome's identification. She mentioned that SNAPS fulfilled most of the criteria of an idiopathic symptom and, when Richard's mouth dropped open, she explained that this meant it had no known cause. She told him she needed him to help her establish a connection between the environment and whatever it was that had caused the condition.

'Ri-ight,' said Richard. 'I think I understand. Are you saying that this is a process of elimination thing?'

Lauren nodded. Richard put a cigarette to his lips, took it out. He sat back, folded his arms and told Lauren that he needed a minute. An hour was more like it. He was a little bit drunk and a little bit disoriented, his understanding out-of-whack. Lauren's request had been dispassionately put. Yet there was also something potty about the situation that didn't quite tie in with her sombre attitude. He wondered whether she wasn't a professor after all, but lived in an underpass and shouted at pigeons.

'I'll have to get back to you on this,' he said.

Lauren watched as Richard wove his way out of the pub. She was glad that was over. It would have been uncomfortable enough without the inappropriate choice of venue. Then again, many things had unsettled her today and not all of them were connected to the pathology of SNAPS itself.

The problem was a simple one. However far she was going to go with her investigations into the syndrome, Lauren would have to deal with death. For years now, she had been practised at remaining detached from such complex emotional engagements. Her work helped, of course, and photography too. But she knew that if she was pulled close enough, the consolation she sought in the application of logic, the secure constraints of order, would not be enough. Nothing would be enough. Because death was always more. Death was the explanation that lay beyond, the reason that hid in the dark. The action out of shot.

Lauren shivered in the busy throb of the bar, suddenly aware she was on her own. In a conscious effort to manage her discomfort, she thought back to the bookseller and what he might be able to do for her.

He seemed enthusiastic enough, albeit in a manner she found a little confrontational. And of course, in commenting on the author the victim had been reading in Corfu, he'd already demonstrated his powers of observation. On a personal level, however, she was not convinced. The prospect of working closely with the man – of establishing the closeness that was a requirement of any successful working relationship – did not appeal. Not that this was entirely his fault. Lauren knew she could be uncomfortable around men; intimacy was not her thing, not any more.

Gosh.

There was no escaping it. Lauren was unwilling to engage with death and loath to consider intimacy for the simple reason that when she did she was taken back. To a lover and a state of mind that were long gone. To Will and the parts of her that he had taken with him when he'd gone.

Will.

Sweet Will.

Sweet Will.

Gosh.

After all this time, was this all it took?

A short story is rejected

Arriving home that night, Richard was still unsure what he had to offer Lauren. Fortunately, the answer made a present of itself. It came in the form of a self-addressed A4 envelope, inside which was a short story and a small printed slip of paper.

'Dear Mr Angry, Thank you for giving us the opportunity to look at your work. Unfortunately we do not think it is quite suitable for *Cutting Edge* magazine and are returning it to you along with a subscription form for the magazine. We wish you luck with placing it elsewhere and thank you again for your interest.'

The rejection was unsigned. Richard poured himself a tot of his weekday whisky and read it again, his head awash with conflicting feelings of resignation and defiance.

The bastards. How dare they knock him back? Who did they think they were? He'd remember this when they came running to him in the future, begging him for a story or yet another mention on The Bilious Bibliophile – they'd not get a word out of him. Then again. He had wondered about that passage, the bit where the narrative voice came down quickly through the gears, switching from the third person to the second to the first in half a page. Then there was the stanza he had written when he was off his chump, slowing the tempo down, playing with the idea of abandoning the narrative thread. He'd taken it out of some drafts, worried that it was too oblique, too demanding. But no. It was just grown-up fiction for Christ's sake, meant for grown-up readers.

And what about the rejection slip? Quite why that was so impersonal, Richard couldn't fathom. It wasn't as if he hadn't sent them stuff in the past. Several times, come to think of it. A chapter of automatic writing, a series of epigrammatic haikus. Well, that was it. He wasn't going to send them any more.

Richard was finished. In the febrile small hours he'd often entertained the idea that his writing would one day be discovered. That he'd sell half a dozen short stories that introduced and then discarded at least three idiomatic anti-conventions. That he would make himself an alternative career, which didn't rely on the vagaries of the reading population at large but on those who knew what they were talking about.

It wasn't going to happen.

There was nobody out there with the balls to publish him, no one who would take a punt on prose as incendiary as his. *Cutting Edge* was supposed to be dedicated to publishing challenging prose, 'transgressive' fiction. Some of the stuff he'd read in there, Christ, he'd had more transgressive pickled eggs of a Sunday lunchtime. More suited to *Woman's Own* it was, or the myriad corporate pedlars of life-free, ambition-light writing that raised mediocrity to a whole new level and served less as stimulation for the intellect or senses than as a culturally cognitive... dimmer... switch...

★

My God.

Richard sat down on the edge of his bed. *Could it be?* The idea was batshit crazy, mad professor stuff. And yet it might prove to be a validation of all that he'd drunk and sweated this last six years.

He rang Lauren, left a message.

'It's the books,' he said.

An author faces his public

The author caught the tube and went walkabout. He walked through the carriages like a mid-thirtysomething man looking for women in a nightclub, with passengers in the role of the potential victims of his chat-up lines. He was looking for something. Five years ago, he'd have been sure to have found it. This time, his first time in a long time, he hadn't yet hit paydirt. But it was surely only a matter of time.

As part of the author's new deal, his first three novels had been reissued as a single volume. 'Reprinted, repackaged and re-presented to a whole new readership.' It was a perfect storm of opportunity. He glanced at his expensive slimline watch. He saw then what he had come to see. It was a man sitting quietly in the corner of a carriage, reading a brightly covered book. It was that very same single volume.

The author paused, brushed himself down and, with a look of surprise playing at the corners of his mouth and a glint in his eye, he approached his quarry, metaphorically licking his lips.

'Hello,' he said. 'I'm Gary Sayles. The very same. I couldn't help noticing you were reading one of my books. Would you like me to sign it for you? Only I've got another one coming out soon. Yes, yes, that's right. I'm making a long-awaited comeback...'

And he was.

And how!

Male confessionals, dad and lad lit

Earlier that day, Gary Sayles had laid down a couple of interviews. The first was for *Man*, a monthly lifestyle magazine packed with Russell Brand, Jeremy Clarkson and TV Celebrity Chef James Martin. He'd been photographed astride a Spacehopper while smoking a pipe, a publicity shot that encapsulated what he was about. The questions had centred around the difficulties – or otherwise – of dressing to impress the ladies in a recession.

The second was an altogether more serious affair. It was about his return to the fictional big time and the themes and inspirations that would catapult him back to the top of the Premier League of contemporary fiction. Hopefully without the need for a word-based penalty shootout. It was going to run in the *Sunday Express* the week after his new book came out. He'd answered the questions with a little bit of honesty, just the right amount of self-confidence and an eye for the main chance, and it had proved to Gary – if proof were needed – that he still had the old magic.

'Why the comeback?' he'd been asked. A potentially tricky question for someone in his position who hadn't got a string of bestselling titles under his belt and who knew their way around a digital tape recorder. But meat and drink for Gary.

'I think that five years is long enough without a new Gary Sayles, don't you? No, no, but seriously. A lot has happened since I wrote my last book. The world has changed. There's been a recession. And I have a responsibility as a writer. I think that as a writer it's important to respond to what's going on in the world.'

'So you think that novelists still have a role to play?' the interviewer had asked. 'Oh yes,' Gary had replied. And he saw that this had hit home and pressed home his advantage. 'You see, I've got a unique relationship with my readers, something that no one else has got. We've grown up together. I've given them pleasure and advice, I've made them laugh. I've shown men how to love. I've even – and this isn't me being falsely modest just for the sake of it – given people someone to look up to.

'The thing is, we've been on a real journey together. And it's important I'm not just there for the good times but the difficult times as well. I want my readers to know that when something unpleasant happens, they can turn to me and I'm still there for them. They need that, you see. Someone to offer them reassurance in a world gone mad.'

'I see. And so how would you describe *The Grass is Greener*?'

'Well, it's actually a bit of a departure for me. As a writer, I think you have to respond to what is going on in the world and so *The Grass is Greener* deals with more serious issues than my first three bestselling titles. In a more mature way. It's still funny, of course, but it touches on themes that affect us all in these straitened times.'

'I see. And these themes...?'

'It's about a writer having a midlife crisis.'

'I'm sorry?'

'A writer having a midlife crisis.'

'A writer? Having a midlife crisis?'

'That's right. It's a good idea, isn't it? There's a lot of scope there for exploring some of the more tricky situations that life can throw up. And besides, I'd said all there was to say about young men growing up, the trials and tribulations of twentysomething friendship, imminent parenthood, whether or not you should have sex with a friend of the opposite sex. So commercially speaking, the time was right for me to move on as well.'

'I see. And, er, do you think you'll carry your readership with you? Or is there a danger that it will be too unsettling for some of your readers?'

'Not really. That's not what my writing's about. When I say I provide comfort for my readers, I mean it. I think it's very important actually. For too long, the world of literature has been dominated by so-called writers who set out to sabotage the fabric of our society. People who think that it's OK to have a go at what makes us tick, to glamorise all that's wrong about human behaviour in the name of lowlife or elitist entertainment. You know the sort. They think it's clever to be cynical and pessimistic. They're desperate to see how far they can go, how low they can stoop. Violence, incest, drug-taking, kidnapping, it's all fair game. Their attitude is wrong. It's corrosive. Because what are books for unless they address the concerns of ordinary people and what they're interested in?

Girlfriends, the problems of living together, wives, pop music, football, going down the pub, *Star Wars*, everyday things. And then growing older, struggling with ageing, turning into a grumpy old man. Moving on to *The Empire Strikes Back* if you like. And not written to impress either, but written in everyday language. That's what books should be about.

'I've always been criticised for being a conventional writer. And I've never quite worked out why convention gets such a bad press. I'll tell you something about conventions. Conventions are there for a reason. They're the fabric of society. What keeps us together. Birth is conventional, death is conventional, and yes, believe it or not, marriage is conventional too. It's the way we do things, the way we've decided is the best. I get really annoyed when people attack convention. What would we put in its place? Go on. Tell me. All these people with their ideas about how we could do things better: you don't see them happy. I tell you, all the unhappiness in the world is caused by ideas. This mess we're in now is caused by so-called intellectuals. People pushing the envelope. Why can't we just accept what we are? Accept that there's a right way to do things? Convention works. If it didn't it wouldn't appeal. It wouldn't be conventional. The way I see it, people are tired of extremes. What they need is to be reassured that there's no shame in the middle of the road.

'That's my response to the mess the world is in. Sticking to what we know works. So no, it won't be too unsettling. I was proud to call my old books conventional. And I'm proud to call my new one conventional too.

'I'm really pleased with the way it's come out as well. Not that that's important. It's what my readers think that matters. Read it. Tell me what you think. I'll be interested to hear.'

It was almost as if he hadn't been away...

Amy

When he got home that night, Gary's wife Amy was sitting in the front room of their Notting Hill terrace. The room was high-ceilinged, white-walled, beech-floored. The sofa was black leather. Amy was listening to a novel on the radio. Their five-year-old son, Garfield, was sprawled on a rug, doodling in an activity book. Gary had arrived home later than Amy had expected. The man on the train had asked for a mention in his next book. Gary had missed his stop but not a marketing opportunity when he decided to dedicate his new novel to 'Everyone I've met on the tube'.

Amy and Gary had been married for ten years. This latest incarnation of their relationship had begun fifteen years ago, at a Coldplay gig at the Warwick Arts Centre. Amy had been working behind the bar and Gary had come from London for the night. He'd barrelled up the M1 armed with an eight-tog quilt and some chat from the magazine where he spent every Saturday de-lidding lattes. He had hoped that the girls of Warwick University would swoon at a local boy making it big in the Smoke. When he'd no-wow-hi-ed into Amy he was delighted. He'd said: 'I'm not going to let you go this time.' The following weekend he'd made the trip again. This time Amy was waiting for him. They had been inseparable ever since.

Their reunion had been a long time coming. It was

the defining encounter in a relationship that stretched back to their time together at infant school in Kings Heath, Birmingham. They'd played kiss chase at five, mothers and fathers at six, hide-and-seek at seven. Gary had first popped the question when they were eight. He'd presented Amy with a thought-that-counts necklace of daisies he'd painstakingly put together during a particularly taxing English lesson.

After junior school, they fell out of touch with one another. They slalomed and scrabbled their way through adolescence and, at eighteen, Gary moved down south to study for a degree in journalism at the University of North London. Amy found herself drawn to an English course and the masochism of the life of a student in Coventry. When they met up again, the time was right. Amy was ready.

As for Gary, it really was a fairytale come true. Amy was the girl next door, his childhood sweetheart, The One. And Gary believed.

That night, as he stood in the living room, Amy could tell instantly that there was something wrong.

'Are you OK, honey?' she asked.

'Yes, Flopsy Bunny,' said Gary, distracted. 'It's just been a long day. I'm fine.'

But he wasn't. That night, the gleam that shone in his eye in the presence of his family had a new intensity. For on his way home, Gary Sayles had been thinking about his new book. And Gary Sayles had had an idea.

★

The next morning Gary leapt out of bed and slipped into his dressing gown. He fetched Garfield a glass of juice. Garfield drank the drink in bed with his mother. While she read to their son, Gary went downstairs to fix breakfast for the three of them. He tried to do this every other weekday. It was the same as always: cornflakes followed by rindless back bacon, toasted sandwich-cut bread and a boiled egg.

The family ate around a pine table in the kitchen. The kitchen was wide and pale and shiny with stainless steel. The units were German and the drawers closed softly and without too much assistance. Gary had chosen the drawers. He'd also chosen the ceramic fruit in the bowl on the side by the silver-finish fridge. And the pasta feature – different shapes, in a glass jar – and the IKEA prints on the wall and the decorative bottle of olive oil that sat next to the cooker. Gary's personality was all over the house. Like the Fresh Smell of Summer Meadows. This was OK. There was no clash there. Amy's personality was elsewhere.

Amy ate her cornflakes. She watched Gary as he wolfed down his barely browned toast. She peeled Garfield's egg and cut his bacon into strips. The egg was runnier than usual. Gary finished his meal and disappeared upstairs for his shower. Half an hour later, while Amy was reading to Garfield, Gary came downstairs. He was dressed for business in his favourite cords/polo shirt combo. He kissed the two of them goodbye and left the house.

Amy looked at the clock. It was half past eight. That was unusual. Irrespective of his work schedule, she always sat with Gary in front of the end of ITV's breakfast show which finished at nine. Gary had appeared on it once. He liked the banter between the hosts. Amy didn't actually watch the programme but the ritual had replaced their five-minute early-morning cuddle which had replaced their ten-minute early-morning lovemaking. Clearing up the dishes, Amy scraped Gary's crusts into the kitchen bin. The bin was full. It was bin day and Gary had left without taking the rubbish out.

Her husband was obviously distracted by something. He'd been distracted all morning. And Amy had first noticed he was behaving oddly last night. She smiled. Bless him. He was off again.

'What's daddy up to?' Amy asked Garfield, 'what's got to daddy now?'

'Daddy can't hear you, silly,' said Garfield. 'Daddy's not here.'

'I know honey,' said Amy. 'But I wonder where he's gone?'

An author grows the brand

Gary Sayles was a man with a lot on his mind. It was as though he had just discovered his first grey nostril hair while looking into a mirror on his thirty-fifth birthday. Because today was the day he went public with his idea.

That morning he had a meeting with his agent, Norwenna, and his editor, Katie, at the HQ of his publisher, Barker Follinge. Normally Gary had been known for his punctuality: on this occasion he thought he'd let them know who was boss and arrived ten minutes after the appointed hour.

He met the two ladies in a conference room on the sixth floor. There was a long table in the room and a flip chart. He noticed his rider – a can of Dr Pepper, not too cold, a bowl of Cheesy Wotsits and one of his signed photos, in a frame – was already in pride of place. The girls were obviously keen to get started.

'Hello, Gary! Good to see you,' said Katie. 'You're looking very well!'

Gary smiled inwardly. She'd got into the habit of opening their meetings with an observation like this but on this occasion, she was right. He nodded enigmatically and transferred his smile to his face.

'Excellent!' said Katie. 'OK. Before we start, then, I'd just like to run through the final touches.'

Gary approved. Whatever masterstroke he was going to drop on them today, it was nice to observe the usual courtesies and the manuscript always came first. By now this final honing of a manuscript was a ritual to him, like watching *Match of the Day*. Historically it took about four meetings and this was the fourth with the new book. Soon it would be ready to be unleashed on an unsuspecting but grateful world.

'At the risk of repeating what I said last time,' continued Katie, 'I have to say that it's looking very good. I think the shift to an older, wiser Gary Sayles really suits you. I mean, I really do think you're going from strength to strength as a writer. There's more *substance* to this one somehow. In fact I only have a few more suggestions to make. Nothing structural – I think the changes we agreed earlier work really well – but there's one or two things we can still do to tighten up the prose in the last thirty pages. Do you have a copy of the manuscript with you?'

'Come now,' chided Gary. 'You should know by now that it's all in here.' He tapped the side of his head with one of his fingers.

'Of course!' said Katie. 'And thank goodness for that! Righty-ho. So there's a section on page two hundred and forty that's the same as one on page two hundred and forty-three. I don't know if you meant to repeat yourself for effect? No? OK, I thought not. Page two hundred and forty-two: it's a "very hot day without a cloud in the sky" when Lucy and her gay friend – what's his name again? – ah yes, Fabrice – arrive for their heart-to-heart; when they come out they're jumping in puddles. So I've altered that slightly. Ah yes. Page two hundred and forty-five. Now I've had some interesting focus group feedback about this passage...'

'Some interesting what?'

'Focus group feedback. A few people have been helping us with the demographic profiling for your new novel. Well, they're not sure about Ben kicking his dog. What's its name? Tyson. They say it's not suitable for the market we're targeting.'

'But he's having a midlife crisis!'

'I agree, Gary, to an extent...'

'... and Tyson's a fighting dog!'

'A Yorkshire terrier, yes, Gary. But this isn't *American Psycho*. And I think they felt it didn't quite ring true. Maybe if Tyson doesn't knock over one of Ben's children "like a skittle with a bowling ball"?'

'I'm not too sure—'

'—it's just that they do have a real understanding of feel-good fiction... and they're all such fans of yours...'

'Well. I suppose I can agree to that,' said Gary, 'but only because I know they know what they're talking about.'

'Good point, Gary, well put! Now. Where were we? Ah yes. Page two hundred and forty-seven: I think we can lose the "silently" from "she shrugged silently". Page two hundred and forty-eight... Ah yes. I'm going to be honest with you here. I think the list is great. I like what you do with lists. Because – let's face it – and Norwenna will back me up here – Norwenna? – it is exactly the way men think. And it's a trademark of yours, isn't it? I remember it from your earlier works. It's just that twenty things on the list is maybe one or two too many.'

'Hmmm. I suppose so. I can always use the last few again. The next time. Maybe in a different context...'

'Exactly! Brilliant! I think that's a very good point. That's another of your gifts that you've obviously honed, your ability to recontextualise material! And it reminds me. Next up we have page two-fifty. Up until this point, I've managed to keep the number of cliché... of easily recognisable phrases down to what we agreed: two per page. And don't get me wrong, I don't think we can afford to skimp on them. It's this ratio that makes you unique. There's no one else even attempting these percentages. And it certainly has implications for brand loyalty. But between page two hundred and fifty and two hundred and sixty we're up to three or four, which may be giving your readers too much of a good thing...'

Gary allowed himself to drift on the sea of Katie's voice. She was one of only a handful of editors still employed at Barker Follinge and the fact that she worked almost exclusively with him was an indication of how big a cheese he was. They'd had their disagreements, of course. Strictly speaking, Katie's background was marketing, not editing, and she'd taken time to adjust to the unique qualities of his writing. On occasion she'd been overly draconian with his prose.

But then he'd had a tricky relationship with everyone who'd worked on his books, even Elizabeth, whom he'd only known for a couple of weeks before she'd died, tragically, during the initial read-through of his new manuscript. The editor for his first three had been Steph and he'd never been sure about her little quirks either. After she'd started work on his debut she'd taken to drinking at odd times of the day, smoking cigarettes. Taking time off because of 'her nerves'. And what kind of 'career move' was it to go from working as the editor of a bestselling author to stopping people in the street – *in the winter!* – and asking them if they'd recently had an accident at work?

'Right, so that's the final few changes, then,' said Katie. 'Now, I've got some news from marketing about the review coverage. Online, we've paid for *I Heart Books*, *Books We Love*, *We Love Books*, *Bookslush*, *Bookchat* and a new site called *Bookchef*. As for print, in keeping with the more serious themes of the novel, we've decided against targeting the usual suspects. So instead of *Ciao!*, *Single!*, *Girlfriend!*, *Spritzer!* and *Bloke*, we're going with *Career Woman*, *Urban Gent*, *Man Hug*, *Pheromone* and *Car*. The supermarkets are all on board. We're not going to go overboard chasing the broadsheets – we've got the *Correspondent* tied in but, frankly, who needs them? – but we're close to finalising a deal with *Metro* and the *Evening Standard*. And I think you saw the review that Mike Parsons has written for the *Mail*? The only issue I have with it is the wording. He's one of ours, you see, and I wondered what you thought about us asking him to change the "funny" to "amusing"? We don't want to be a hostage to fortu... no, no, that's not what I mean. It's just that "funny" can have unfortunate connotations. One person's Chris Evans is another's Stewart Lee.'

'Stewart who?'

'Not your core demographic, Gary, not your core demographic. Anyway, we don't want to frighten the horses, do we?'

'Whatever,' said Gary, suddenly tiring of playing second fiddle to Katie's conductor. 'Look, do what you have to. I trust you. OK? Now I want to tell you about my idea.'

And so then Gary outlined his plan. Throughout, he kept an eye on the responses of his audience. Katie looked confused, like a lady who'd long since given up trying to understand the offside rule. Norwenna was her usual sphinx-like self. Gary was never sure what Norwenna was thinking. Sometimes he would catch her staring out of the window, as if she was imagining which colour of Spangles she was going to choose.

When he had finished explaining, he waited for the ladies' responses.

'I can see it. I think. Yes, yes, I can,' said Katie. For the first time in her life, she looked nervous.

'I think it's a great idea, Gary,' agreed Norwenna, reminding Gary of what she brought to the table. 'It's brave, yes, but I think you'll be able to carry it off.'

'I knew you'd see it my way,' he said. It was just as well that Barker Follinge were being so welcoming. He had no need to suffer fools, gladly or otherwise. There weren't many who could match his record of three bestselling books in five years. He was one of the few writers capable of tapping into what people wanted and giving it to them. In that respect he was like Mel Gibson in the classic noughties comedy *What Women Want*, only for both sexes. More to the point, he'd done it all the hard way. Not by retiring to an ivory tower and studying English Literature or any of that ridiculous Creative Writing but by working in the real world, struggling along with a Media Studies course and the harsh realities of working on a top twenty magazine.

As far as Gary was concerned, that was the end of the meeting. A journey which had begun ten long years ago with the delivery of his firstborn – conceived in ink and swaddled in a brightly coloured cover – was about to enter another chapter. He was itching to get out into the real world. His wasn't a big idea but now he'd practically demanded the approval of his publisher, he would take it elsewhere, to where it belonged, to the people who bought his books.

And how.

Pippa and Zeke

Pippa and Zeke share a flat that is part Marylebone, part Fitzrovia. They are exhibitionists. Pippa and Zeke have had sex in the Warwick Castle, on the Portobello Road, London Zoo, St Paul's Cathedral, the British Museum and on the 3.15 from Shadwell to Tottenham Court Road (change at Bank). Their penchant for threesomes, foursomes and public displays of masturbation has been noted.

They are in love but their love is not the love of others. They come at it from a different angle. Their love is strapped on. It has attachments.

Pippa and Zeke have no friends. They have acolytes. They socialise with rich kids and posh dealers, porn freaks, adeviants, club whores, fish-fuckers, po-mo bohos, faux homos and snobs. Pippa and Zeke are known by these people for their lifestyle. They dress down and dress sideways to dress up. It is charity-shop chic, once removed. Pippa wears nylon shirts, Crimplene dresses and terry towelling adult Babygros. She often sports a bowler hat that she picked up for a song down the market. Zeke dresses in skirts and fluorescent shirts. To the corner shop for a pint of milk? A two-foot afro wig will suit.

Pippa and Zeke like to party. Their tastes are catholic, exclusive. They smoke imported American organic cigarettes. They take MDMA as powder and liquid GHB. Also pharmaceutically pure acid, the occasional puff of poppy, Special K, hash oil and Cava Cava tea. They drink Veuve Cliquot, Pimm's Cup, Budvar, Cooper's Sparkling Ale, Stolichnaya, Hill's Absinthe and Manhattans. Breakfast is often Bloody Marys made with Marie Sharp's Habanero Sauce, all the way from Belize.

Pippa and Zeke are conceptual artists. They are postmoderns. They draw inspiration from a number of sources. They are a little bit garage, a little bit punk, a little bit trash. Urban, def, vanilla, street. Ideologies, fetishes, traditions, racial insecurities and cultural prejudices are diluted and thickened and then mixed and matched, cut and pasted, applied with post-ironic lack of precision and slapped about with squealish gay abandon. To Pippa and Zeke the world is one second-hand goodie-market of this-and-that and bits-and-bobs, to be cadged or taxed, blown apart, stuck together, pinned up or taken down. It is empty of anything of interest except that which is grist to their hi-tech lo-fi multi-media retro-mill. It is full – absolutely chocka-blocka full – of meh.

But then they are postmoderns. Truth is an untruth and beauty untruth too. Art is a commodity. It has no significance beyond the sales pitch, no consequence beyond the cash. It performs no function. There is nothing beneath the surface. There is space beneath the surface. Should the buyer or critic desire, this space may be filled. You want art to be about stuff? Recession, poverty, riots, anarchism, religion, war, death, sex, happiness, consumerism? Go ahead. Knock yourself out. Cram it in, it's up to you. It's not there, though, not really. Any of it. Because art don't mean shit. The world is full of meh and meaning is a busted flush.

If this doesn't reflect well on Pippa and Zeke, it's worth remembering that they neither make nor break the rules. They are salespeople, that is all. They are good at it too. No one is forcing the punters to buy. Yet Pippa and Zeke make money. People do buy. And people do cram stuff in.

They once exhibited a six-inch model of an Allis-Chalmers Model U Tractor. Writing in the programme, the curator Olivia Verne-Laverne wrote: 'Looking at this piece, you are reminded that the countryside is what it is because of, and not despite, the hand of man.'

Another time, Pippa and Zeke showed a photo-montage in a small gallery that had some pocket behind it and was rumoured to be taxiing for take-off. In the image a doleful fat white woman with a rustic pockholed boat-race is framed against a backdrop of razor-bewired tower blocks. She is wearing a tam and a white smock. She is chewing on a erb stalk. Next to her is a staring black man. He is standing in a picturesque village. Behind him are thatched cottages, Chiltern Hills. He is wearing green wellington boots and the hat of a country bumpkin. He is chewing on a piece of straw. Writing in *Skirtingboard ArtStyleMagazine,* Tom Smyth said of the piece: 'We can only truly say that black and white are nice and tight when we can see works like "Untitled" and are not stopped in our tracks by their primal power.'

Later, Pippa and Zeke lived for a month on diets. For the first week they chose Chapter One of *The Adam and Eve Diet,* for the second Chapter Two of *The Little Black*

Dress Diet. To follow they chose Chapter Seven of *The Waterfall Diet* and to finish they tackled Chapter Five of *The Carbohydrates Diet.* This project earned Pippa and Zeke a ten-minute slot after the news on Channel Four during which they declared that they had lost no weight and were no more nor less happy within themselves than they had been before they had started. An oppo on the *Metro* wrote the listing: 'Short piece which exposes the diet industry for the fat-headed fraud it really is.'

Pippa and Zeke also do the funnies. One time, back in the day, they filmed themselves in oversized skater gear, stopping old people in the street and asking them questions about Christ Grinds and 540 Disasters. Some of them bandy coots don't hear so good. They blogged a series of one-hundred-word fictions about hippopotamuses called Eric or five-year-old girls called Mabel who have qualified as bus drivers and are precociously conversant with the profane argot of the street.

Three of Pippa and Zeke's projects are ongoing. The first is an oblique trolling of an online gardening forum. 'Blackfly? I swear by a liberal coating of Danish Oil. Works every time!'

The second is a contract to compose a selection of a hundred suggested verses for people using the *Evening Post*'s In Memoriam column. To date they have sixty-two. They have snuck some in under the radar. One reads:

'Her life was full of worthy deeds,
Always there for those in need,
True and pure in heart and mind,
A loving memory left behind.'

Another reads:

> 'In God's garden there is no pain,
> And only sometimes a little rain,
> It is full of flowers, in the main.'

Pippa and Zeke are walking home after a party. They are passing through Fitzroy Square, discussing their art. Pippa is wearing a clown outfit and Zeke is dressed as a hippy chick. The city is half asleep. It is late summer and the air is high and thin. It goes all the way up to the fumes and smells sweet and earthy and full of the endless cycles of the day.

Pippa and Zeke pass people walking small dogs, a bench-sitter, someone sitting on the grass. Zeke and Pippa wave cheerily, say, 'GOOD MORNING!'

'Some party,' says Pippa.

'The party to end all parties,' says Zeke.

'And I mean that most sincerely, folks,' says Pippa.

They start to sing.

> 'Our little lamb, so sweet and pure
> Upon this earth did roam.
> But that was fifty years ago
> And now our lamb is loam.

> 'He's a corpse I tell you
> A stiff in a grave
> They plucked out his nostrils
> And gave him a shave.'

'Coming along nicely,' says Pippa.

'It is, it is,' says Zeke.

'This is our time,' says Pippa.

'It is, it is,' says Zeke.

But they are a project light at the moment and Pippa has an idea. 'Religion's all the rage at the moment. Blasphemy, that sort of thing. We should do something that people think is about religion.'

'Like what?'

'I don't know. Skip Allah, tho', eh? Bit close to the bone, that.'

'The wily Pathans?'

'The wily Pathans. How about something potentially Jew-baiting instead? That's always a safe bet. We could turn into Jews and wear skullcaps and clown masks. Or turn into Hindus and then go begging. And not wash. And eat burgers. The atheists'll love that.'

'How do you turn into a Hindu?' says Zeke.

'Don't know. I'll look into it. There has to be a way. Maybe we could go to the Ganges and do it properly...'

'Maybe,' says Zeke.

'... or else head to Nottingham and take a dip in the river there. The Avon as the Ganges of the north. I like it. It's got potential. There are Hindus in Nottingham, aren't there? Or is that Sikhs? Or Leicester. Is there a river runs through Leicester?'

'Maybe,' says Zeke.

'Maybe?' says Pippa. 'Yes maybe, baby, maybe, baby. Maybe sex. We could do sex. Sex and dwarves. "Does Size Matter?" We could find a friendly dwarf and dress it up as Charlotte Charles.'

Charlotte Charles is Pippa and Zeke's favourite vibrator. It is a three-way Rampant Rabbit. It has five rotating patterns and a crude sense of humour. Zeke is happy with the suggestion. But Pippa is not convinced. She is thinking of something with a bit more snark.

They continue on their way.

Richard chats up Lauren

A week after they had met in the pub, Richard arranged to see Lauren at her home. She lived about a mile from his shop, on one of Harborne's more tree-filled streets. The two of them were to discuss his theory and where books might fit into SNAPS.

For Richard, this was a potentially tricky encounter. This part of the suburb – all mossy waist-high walls, over-neat hedging, wide roads and refined, polite, dependable Victorian houses – was off his stomping ground. And sure enough, as he crunched up Lauren's thickly gravelled drive, he was reminded of the knack she seemed to have of nudging him out of the carefully constructed spikiness of his comfort zone.

This time, however, Richard was determined to ignore any distractions that might come his way. It was his fancy for the Prof that mattered tonight, nothing else. It had to be. The last time Richard checked, libertines like him were enjoying sex on an almost daily basis. And it had been a long time since he had managed to get a slice of that particular amorality pie.

So long, in fact, that a more traditionally realistic man might have developed a complex about his lack of sexual success. But in this, if nothing else, Richard was an optimist. Besides, when it came to Lauren the signs were good. During their meeting in the pub he'd noticed the strained formality of her speech, the defensiveness of her body language. In his experience this was the behaviour of a sexual naif and sexual naifs were invariably more susceptible to his chat than those who had heard it all before.

Not to mention her choice of photography as a hobby. It was such a painfully solitary pursuit. What was all that about, unless it was the world's most carefully presented cry for help? The woman clearly needed saving from herself, and he was the man to do it...

To this end, Richard had made a plan. In his experience, his chance of meaningful interference with a woman was directly related to the quantity of alcohol consumed by each party. Notwithstanding the fact that most women would have to get drunk before they'd contemplate braving his rugged masculinity (which sometimes doubled as an Antipodean attention to personal hygiene), he would need it to produce the chat that would seal the deal. Now Richard knew his optimum wit level to be two bottles of wine. But he was no fool. Among those of mediocre intake – and he had Lauren down as one such novice – he knew that two bottles would be considered excessive.

This was where the plan came in. It was a simple plan. Richard was taking two bottles of wine with him to their meeting. After they had drunk the first between them he knew that Lauren would do the done thing and open one of her own. Between them they would therefore have drunk one each. At this point, rather than appear a lush-bum and offer to crack open his second bottle (and the third between them), he would instead offer it up as a gift. A gesture that would simultaneously show his generosity and throw the woman into a handy spin. And to make up the shortfall in the intake required for him to reach his optimum wit level? Why, fuck me if he wouldn't simply polish off a bottle before leaving for their ren-dez-vous.

This he'd duly done, and with his plums replete on his thigh and his head pleasantly abuzz, he rang Lauren's doorbell, blushed Slovenian Cab Sauv at the sight of her and was ushered through a Berber-rugged entrance hall into a living room of dark wood cabinets, tasselled rugs and sofas in mint and jade.

'Before we start,' said Richard, on a roll before he'd begun, 'shall I open this? It's a decent drop of French. None of that New World nonsense that the peasants sink. I thought it would, how you say, get the juices flowing? We could drink to the successful conclusion of our endeavours...'

'Thank you but I won't,' said Lauren.

'Oh,' said Richard. 'Oh, ah, oh.'

'Are you OK?' said Lauren. 'Would you like a glass of water?'

'Yes. I mean no. Are you sure?' said Richard.

'Yes. Thank you. But feel free...'

Richard had to think quickly. Of the relationship between sex and literature and wit and spontaneity and wine.

'OK. Just the one.'

Lauren left the room and returned with a goblet the size of a toilet bowl. 'So,' she said, 'what did you want to tell me about?' Half an hour and two goblets later, Richard was opening his second bottle of the meeting and third of the night and had begun a denunciation of a 'putrid aesthetic fashioned by the barely breathing morality of fools'. It was at this point that Lauren, who until then had seen no alternative to listening politely, cut in.

'I'm sorry, but can I stop you there for a moment? As fascinating as this is, I didn't ask you here for an abstract or theoretical debate about good or bad books. I asked you here because you've advanced an interesting theory about what might be the cause of the syndrome known as SNAPS. Now. When we were in Corfu, you commented on the manuscript the woman was reading when she collapsed. And the book her partner had with him. So. What, specifically, can you tell me about them?'

'Well, the manuscript the woman was reading was a new novel by a bloke called Gary Sayles. The book the man was reading was an omnibus edition of his first three. They must have brought it out to tie in with his new one. Either that or it's the International Year of the Moron.'

'Hmm. And why do you think these novels have something to do with SNAPS? Are you familiar with the author?'

'Do me a favour. I wouldn't touch him with yours. He writes what is known in the trade as "male confessionals". They're books for people can't read.'

'I don't understand.'

'Reading isn't just about forming words in your brain and linking them until they make the first sort of sense. That's what children do. There's more to it than that. It's like writing; there're bad readers and good readers. Male confessionals are for bad readers.

Except, I suppose they are so obviously part of a broader cultural consensus you could allow yourself to be swept away with generosity and suggest they're aimed at the merely mediocre.'

'What do you mean?'

'Put it like this. I believe fiction should make people smart and dribble and blether and snort and gibber and hustle and ogle and fart. It should confront the terrible truths of the world. These books don't. They're all about young men afraid of commitment, middle-aged men having midlife crises. Not that there's anything wrong with writing about marriage or suburban relationships or middle management types per se. But Jeez, it's got to be done well. These aren't. They rely on "recognition", of "the sky was blue" variety. If I'm reading a book, I don't want to be sitting there nodding like a dashboard dog, I want to be gazing in wild surmise. I want to be moved. And by that I don't mean just emotionally manipulated, moved as in chasing my tail. I mean moved as in having my perceptions altered, my perspectives shifted. I want to be made to feel or think differently about life.'

'Yes,' said Lauren, 'I think I get the picture. But to return to the matter in hand, I need something from you. To be precise, I need you to read the books. You said these "male confessionals" might be a contributing factor to SNAPS. Well, leaving aside for the moment your antipathy towards them, I don't have any evidence to support this assertion. So I need to establish if there is something in the texts. Some peculiar combination of words or themes maybe. Something unique to this genre.'

'I've already told you. There is. They're the biggest sack of sh—'

'—Yes, thank you. I heard. But this has to be an objective analysis.'

'I'm not sure they'd stand up to much analysis. They're just formulaic pus. The lowest common denominator—'

'Wait! You said formulaic. You mean there's some kind of formula?'

'Yes. But then most novels have a formula. It's just that some are more two plus two than E=MC squared. In this case, I'm not convinced that we need to nail the specifics. Isn't it enough that they're so generically bad? That was what I meant when I said it was the books. I mean the quality of the writing in these things is enough to send anyone off to the big sleep.'

'The big sleep? It's *death* we're talking about here. Two people have lost their lives.'

Richard, who was still puppy-dog grateful for the opportunity to air his 'putrid aesthetic' chat, nearly allowed the implications of Lauren's news to pass him by.

'Yes, yes, I get it. Death. Very bad, yes. And I'm going to have to look at the books for you... Hang on a minute. Did you say two people have died? I thought it was just one?'

Lauren smiled and the thought occurred to Richard that she had been testing him, making sure he was paying attention. She told him that a British consular official who had helped with the investigation into the first death had himself later fallen victim to the syndrome. Not only that, but having spoken to the investigating authorities, she had established that he had 'borrowed' the manuscript from the first victim and had been reading it when he'd died.

'Well, if these books really are the cause of this SNAPS, isn't that a flaw in your plan?' said Richard. 'If I read them, who's to say that *I* won't cark it? Come to think of it, why can't you read them yourself?'

'Two reasonable points. Please let me explain. Firstly, although SNAPS has been called a spontaneous condition, it almost certainly isn't. Think of it as a stroke. The axonal degradation that leads to the syndrome is caused by either long-term or concentrated exposure to whatever it is that compromises their continued function. Or look at it this way: as you say, this author's first three books were bestsellers and yet this is the first anyone has heard of SNAPS. So despite the fact that their contents may help me to identify a causal link, it is extremely unlikely that reading the first three books in isolation – that is, with a large enough gap between each one – will have a deleterious effect on your brain function. Secondly, it's been a long time since I read any fiction. You, I presume, read it all the time. And will therefore see patterns in the text that I may miss.'

'OK, OK, you're the boss,' said Richard. 'Could you tell me where your toilet is, please?'

Michael Kruger.
And Lauren's books

Richard left the room and smeared off the walls of the quarry-tiled hall. Although the whole SNAPS thing was proving to be a bit of a mind-fuck, his chat had been nothing if not triple-distilled and the night was going well. It was just a shame she wasn't drinking.

Unsure of the directions Lauren had just given him, Richard opened the first door he saw. It led to a room under the stairs and a set of steps that led down to darkness. He contemplated having a look. There was definitely some comedy value in mentioning to Lauren that he had taken a wrong turn, missed the light switch and pissed in the mop bucket... no, maybe not. Not yet at any rate. He tried the second door. It opened easily and he walked in and switched on the light. This wasn't right either. He was standing in a small back room. It was the sort of room you'd find in many Victorian houses: dried grasses and a sunflower head sat in a vase on top of a black iron fireplace that faced the door; above the mantelpiece was a framed print of a pre-Raphaelite piece in which some wafty woman was getting wet. On his right, a pair of French windows looked out over a whitewashed and land-scaped patio. A wall covered in books was on his left. Richard took a step back.

On the shelves closest to him sat academic stuff, a collection of box files and ring-backed scientific journals. There were reference books on birds and flowers and landscape photography, another on architecture. It was those titles farther along the wall that caught his attention and caused him to whistle

For some people, sexual attraction is distilled in the way someone walks. For others it is the way they talk. With Richard – at least since Julie had sauntered provocatively off, mouthing unanswerables, a copy of *The Da Vinci Code* in her hand – it was what they read. And while he'd speculated long and hard about her tastes, this was the first time he'd had the opportunity to make any sort of connection between Lauren and the books she read.

There was nothing there that was heinous – all of the books were worthy of his cautious approval – but there was something odd about the collection. It was filled with titles that didn't seem to fit with what little he knew of Lauren's approach to art and life. Were these really the books of the woman who spoke in conversation as though she was addressing a roomful of hard-of-thinking students?

His dealings with her to date had certainly given no indication of a romantic streak or an interest in classic verse or history. And yet here was poetry from Edmund Spenser, Coleridge and Keats. He saw *The Arabian Nights* and *The Bride of Lammermoor* and the letters of Madame de Sévigné. There was some Dante, Chaucer and Homer, a biography of John Donne, Roberto di Ridolfi's *Life of Savonarola*, then more verse from Henry Vaughan, Richard Crawshaw and Thomas Traherne. A copy of Charlotte Guest's *Mabinogion* sat next to some sonnets from Pierre de Ronsard and pride of place, in the middle of the wall, went to all nine volumes of Herodotus's *Histories*.

None of them were new editions. Judging by the fraying spines and exposed stringiness, not one of them was under twenty years old. And yet despite their disrepair, they didn't appear to have been recently disturbed. They weren't well used. Quite the opposite, in fact. Rooms filled with books should be alive, if only with a mocking of death. This one wasn't. It was as still and sad as an empty pub.

There was another thing. The titles in the collection didn't seem to belong together. Some seemed almost wilfully obscure. It was almost as if they'd been chosen for effect, as an ostentatious yet witless display of erudition. For the first time that night, Richard felt uncomfortable, as though he was missing something.

He found the bathroom at the third time of asking. As he flopped his cock he mulled over what he had just seen. It was all very confusing. He decided that he would raise the matter when he'd had more time to work on a riff. He went back to the living room, anxious to return to less boggy ground.

'Where were we?' he said. 'Oh, I remember. The appliance of science. I could come up with a Banality Rating if you like. How about: 1–3 – Read it Before; 4–6 – Not Remotely Enthralling; 6–8 – Danger of Dozing; 8–10 – Yawnsnoozecoma...'

'Right. So that's... how many bottles of wine now? Two? Three?'

'Why, thank you.'

'If you don't mind me asking such a personal question – and I'm guessing you don't – why do you drink so much? Every time I see you, you are the worse for wear.'

'Aha! I'm glad you asked. It's interesting that. There's this poet, a German fella called Michael Kruger, who once wrote: "Someone who reads too much without wetting his whistle regularly will become stupid; someone who drinks too much without diluting his drink with literature will end up in the gutter. Only the two together preserve culture; only the two together are culture." And that – right there – is the way I look at things. What do you think of that?'

'It's a nice sentiment,' said Lauren, 'and you've certainly done well to remember it word for word. But even though it's all very well throwing yourself into these things, you need to keep a sense of who you are, a sense of perspective. Otherwise you get lost. And, since you ask, I'm not too sure that one's appreciation of culture is necessarily enhanced by being permanently drunk.'

'Do you know something, Lauren, I'm not going to lie to you. As you might have gathered, I'm a man of extremes. I'm drawn to the edges of things. For me, that's where the interesting stuff is. And drinking's a part of that.'

'I see.'

'Don't get me wrong. I'm not dissing you. I'm just trying to – how you say – establish a paradigm, make sure we understand each other. Don't set out on the wrong foot. Speaking of which,' said Richard, flashing her a seductive leer that he'd been practising all week and now got half right, 'I was wondering if, you know, you might like to discuss this over a meal some time?'

'I think that's probably enough for tonight, don't you?' said Lauren, and with that she stood up and gestured towards the door. 'Thanks for your help. I'll be in touch when I've had a chance to think about what we've discussed.'

Cavorted and gambolled...

Richard left. The gravel on Lauren's drive was fun to walk on. He walked out and into and down the middle of the road and whistled. Looked up at the moon. The wine had gone. All of it. He hadn't succeeded. With Plan A or Plan B or whatever plan it was. He'd been distracted again. It didn't matter. It wasn't about the sex. Who was he trying to kid? He saw a stone in the road. Aimed a kick at it. Missed. Went back and tried again. He'd drunk all the wine. All that planning and he'd drunk all the wine. It didn't matter. Not really. I mean. Whose chain was he yanking? The stone cavorted down the road. Cavorted and gambolled and skipped. He started to sing a song. By the Pogues. Wasn't too sure which one. He looked at the hedges on either side of the road. They were tall. Harborne was nice. Nice. It didn't matter. Nothing wrong with nice. Once in a while. Not that he'd let that slip. No, he'd held it together. Stayed bad. After two bottles of wine, after three bottles of wine, he'd held it together. Men like him were a dying breed. Raging against the mightiness of the dim. Hey. That was quite good that. If only she knew. Lauren. Lau-ren. Ah, Lauren. *Lauren*. What a woman! She was so... so... So what, actually? Sexy? Not ex-actly. It didn't matter. Really it didn't matter. He was kidding nobody. As long as she knew how good he was. With words. The truth. About him.

And his words. And the wine. And the way he felt.
If only she knew the truth about the wine.

Richard was drunk.

And Richard was in love.

Towards emotional literacy

Lauren watched Richard stumble into the rowan. He was an infuriating man, full of desperation and frantic need. For what, she couldn't tell, and she wondered whether he knew himself. Whatever it was, it didn't bode well for their working relationship.

In her mind's eye she framed him against the bush, zoomed in, held him there. But then a strange thing happened. She didn't take the picture. Somehow it was not enough. She thought again of Will, and her memories came to her like rays of sunlight, fragile yet insistent and dazzling and beautiful still...

It was sixteen years ago now. They had met at university a month into the first term of the first year, at the inaugural meeting of the ill-starred Society for the Appreciation of Local Architectural Beauty. Will was studying literature. He was a poet and contributing editor of the first-year poetry newsletter. His father was a classics professor and his mother an archaeologist and he had been educated at a private school just along from the university. Lauren was studying biochemistry. She had gone to a local grammar school at which her mother had taught geometry. It was from her that Lauren had inherited her love of architecture. Aside from this, she and Will had few interests in common but he was curly haired and brown eyed and when he spoke he sounded unlike anyone that

Lauren had ever met, his voice rich with expectation and promise. And she knew she would never feel this way about anyone again.

That first autumn, as they sat on the grass in the shadow of the campus clock tower, he had read to her from the metaphysical poets. Carried away by the moment, he'd brushed her medium-length hair into and out of her eyes and told her she was 'pale and interesting' and that she was the muse he had yearned for throughout his adolescence. They'd giggled at this and then his hand had touched her thigh and they had both started.

Later, they'd made love with studied abandon and Will had talked of the circles of life and death and of the journeys that they would take and then he had read to her some more. He read to her often, yellowing snippets of poetry and prose, his words providing the rhythm of their days and nights.

As she listened to his voice, the whole world was a whirr and a fizz, pregnant with possibilities and clues, bursting with the unknown. Lauren found herself alive in the words of one poem in particular, 'First Love', by John Clare. Will had found it in a second-hand Penguin and knew pieces of it by rote:

I ne'er was struck before that hour
With love so sudden and so sweet,
Her face it bloomed like a sweet flower
And stole my heart away complete.

Are flowers the winter's choice?
Is love's bed always snow?

She seemed to hear my silent voice,
Not love's appeals to know.

I never saw so sweet a face
As that I stood before,
My heart has left its dwelling place
And can return no more.

They were young then and on the occasions when
Lauren had been unable to stop herself from looking
back, she'd realised they had wasted all the things
that the young are obliged to waste, like seriousness,
levity and time. Especially time. For the most part,
time passed in a miasmic blur of reading, listening,
lovemaking, watching old films, dreaming. Right up
until the day it stopped.

Two summers into their relationship they went
out for a Sunday afternoon drive in the countryside
around Hay-on-Wye. They drove through blooming
cider orchards, a wicker basket in the boot. In the
town, they stopped for a perusal of flaky books and
then, gently spurred by hunger, wound along shady
lanes to find a place for a picnic. They parked on
a road by a brook which ran through a blushing
meadow and Lauren remembered they had to walk
some minutes to find a patch of grass that was dry
enough to sit on.

They were in no rush. When they found the ideal
spot, next to a clump of vivacious red campion, they
spread a blanket and lay on the ground. Will picked
cowslips and buttercups and rubbed their heads gently
down Lauren's bare arms and along the thin veins

in her wrists and he touched them to her lips. She ruffled his hair and they kissed. The sun was high. It was pleasingly hot. The light was lazy and long, stretching the afternoon around the curve of the earth they shared.

They ate village-baked pastries. Will made short work of a small crusty pork pie, thinly sliced with an old penknife and slathered with French mustard. Lauren nibbled at a leek and potato bake and then they each had a piece of a Normandy apple tart with a funny little lattice on top.

Will opened a half bottle of Taittinger Reserve and they drank slowly as they sat. They had a conversation about the size of the bubbles. Neither of them drank very much and the alcohol went straight to their heads. They dozed blissfully until the early evening air grew thinner and then Will said something to Lauren, probably 'let's pull chocks' or 'let's paint our wagon', she was never quite sure of what exactly he'd said at that moment, and then they were sitting in the car again and cutting through the dusk and heading back to the city.

Lauren was driving with Will sitting next to her. As she drove through the oranges and greens and yellows and reds of the last country light she felt happy but also – she thought she remembered this clearly – also strangely melancholy, as though she realised that something had ended and this was as happy as she was ever going to feel.

It was Lauren's first car and on the way to Hay Will had jokingly suggested that he write her a poem, 'An Ode to the Maestro of an Austin'. Lauren had agreed because he had with him a pen that she had bought for his twentieth birthday not a week before and he had not yet used it to compose anything for her. Now he sat and wrote, the two of them in perfect silence. Cresting the brow of a dip, Lauren took her eyes off the road for an instant as she turned to look at him. He was stroking the side of his nose with the pen, his profile sharp and distinguished, curls of hair against his neck. She smiled, her eyes misty with love. By the time she turned back to the road there were only trees and green leaves. Lauren hit the brakes and then the trunk of an Orange Pippin. Will pitched forward. His head hit the dashboard. The pen disappeared.

Lauren remembered the blood, dripping down her nose and metallic in her mouth. And as she drifted in and out of consciousness, she remembered the blood that seeped from the mouth of her lover.

She spent five days in hospital suffering from concussion and shock. When she came out she was consumed by a ravening anguish. It wasn't the 'how' that taxed her, that kept her awake at nights and folded up during the day. It was the 'why'. She knew that Will had died because he had lodged a Parker Inflection Rollerball up his nose with sufficient force to enter his brain: it was just that try as she might she couldn't see where his death fitted into any equation or number of equations she'd known. Instead it seemed to be a glimpse into an alien world, a world of little or no order. A world of emotional complexity in which what she felt led into a darkness that could not be illuminated by science. A world she had had no intention of visiting again.

At first she'd tried to cope in the traditional way. His parents were absolute bricks, of course, and she'd stayed in touch with them. At one point she took to writing things down in a notebook – her recollection of the events of the day, some of the things she thought he'd said to her about their future. Later, in her third year, in an attempt to find a belief system and an individual to assuage the hurt and guilt, she had turned to the East. His name was Melvin and he was a t'ai chi instructor from just outside Norwich. They were together for six months. It seemed to be working out. She could feel herself making progress, beginning to appreciate her feelings from an objective distance. Then Melvin met someone who knew as much t'ai chi as he did. She showed him some moves, he showed her some moves, and Lauren sat at home in the lotus position, centred and alone.

After that Lauren had simply given up. She cut herself off from people. More to the point, she tried to cut herself off from how she felt and had felt about Will. In place of these feelings she kept only the snapshots she had taken and the books his parents had given to her when he'd died. Heirlooms, old books she hadn't read and had no time to read. His life in a filing system in chronological order, sitting unloved on bookcases, the paper turning from cream to yellow, the lines of text growing less bold, like wraiths draining of energy. That was all she had left of Will and all that she needed. She would stick to what made sense, to an existence of emotional stasis. The rest was simply too much to bear. There was just one concession: 'First Love', transcribed for her by him and kept in an inlaid rosewood chest of drawers beside her cotton-sheeted and wistfully king-sized bed...

It was easy for Lauren to withdraw into herself. Her social life at the university was restricted to drinks in the pub with other members of the photographic society, and the odd attempt at matchmaking from imaginative fellow students who clung to a belief that beneath her stand-offish exterior there beat the heart of a drama undergraduate. One spring she rekindled a childhood interest in botany – and there had always been birds – but in place of forming genuine friendships and attachments Lauren channelled all of her energies into her studies. She did well. Her emotional atrophy was mistaken by all of her acquaintances for a peculiarly durable level-headedness. And so, detached from the distraction of the mess people were and the mess they made of things, afraid and secure in her ordered and understandable world, Lauren quickly became a success in her field, a field that was substantial enough to provide an adequate diversion from the 'why' that ate away at her heart.

Until this.

Quite without warning, she had found herself sucked into a process that compromised the consolation she found in her work. Her involvement with SNAPS had only just started, yet already her work on the syndrome had exposed her to an environment to which she would not otherwise have been exposed, to fiction, to infuriating people and to behaviours defined by desperation and frantic need. And, of course, to death.

More particularly SNAPS had brought death to Lauren through words and the energy they provided or could take away. And so she found herself drawn again to 'First Love'. She had returned to the poem on many occasions since Will had gone away. First it had been every week, then every month, then whenever she was feeling a little off kilter, either cold in summer or warm in winter, invigorated by autumn or made reflective by spring. The words righted her, gave her comfort and solace. And they were vital. Even as they spoke to her of death they seemed to keep her lover alive. Now, through her exposure to SNAPS and to lives that might have been ended by more quantifiably powerful words, it suddenly seemed to Lauren that the opposite was true. The words had ossified Will, petrified him. And in addition to helping keep her pain at a distance, the poem had also set it in stone.

The memory of Will deserved more than this. And so it was that, as she sat there, in her too-big front room, Lauren came to a decision. It was time for her heart to return to its dwelling place. It was time to let go, to move on, to set Will free and to free herself.

Lauren would grasp the opportunity that SNAPS presented. She would conduct an experiment that would run alongside her professional investigation into the condition. An experiment in which she would engage once again with that which she did not understand and could not order, however unsettling this might at first prove to be. An experiment in which she would expose her cortical network to an environment of such extremes that its very nature could change. An experiment in which she would subject her debilitating emotional atrophy to a sustained and profound interrogation.

An experiment in which Professor Lauren Furrows would leave herself at the mercy of the dark and emotionally complex world of books.

Sacrilege

Richard began reading the single-volume edition of Gary Sayles' first three novels. He read quickly but carefully too, as he was wary of the words. He drank strong coffee to keep himself awake and the finest Waterloo Brandy to help him sleep. Whenever he felt his head becoming too clear, he took brisk walks around the block. He read on the bus, the volume hidden inside copies of *Razzle* or *The Watchtower*, and he read at home, under the covers of his man-crusty duvet. He read at the till point at work and whenever the strong coffee and Waterloo Brandy got the upper hand in the daily battle for control of his anarchic and gippy guts.

As he read, Richard looked for a pattern. He compared chapters, looked at structure, explored shifts in what he presumed was the paradigm. He made a note of frequently occurring words or phrases (these included The One, singleton, twentysomething, thirtysomething, one-night stand (meaningless), one-night stand (significant), significant other (ironic), significant other (non-ironic), record collection, beer, football and small child).

He isolated several factors that could conceivably contribute to a degradation of the brain. There was, for instance, an unquestioning narrative reliance on the acceptance of a peculiarly conservative value system. Accounts of supposed angst that did not compute. The recurrent 'male-in-crisis' theme seemed exaggerated, given what Richard knew of the economics of the gender divide. There also seemed to be an overuse of domestic situations that were of little dramatic interest and consisted instead of observational asides about waiting for plumbers, arguing over the remote control, visiting the dentist, being pasted by a kid on Xbox's *CounterStrike* and the like. Technically, there was the way that Sayles conveyed information in the form of lists, as a way of avoiding stringing sentences together. The way he frequently used Capital Letters merely to emphasise Crucial Moments. Furthermore, on closer examination, each novel could be broken down into a series of only vaguely related lifestyle magazine pieces. And this was not to mention the number of times the author name-checked *Star Wars*.

Of further possible interest to Lauren was the fact that the three of them were essentially the same book, rewritten. On the surface this wasn't so. *Our Legendary Twenties* was about a single twenty-something professional Londoner looking for love. *Cutting the Cake* concerned itself with a late twenty-something professional Londoner unsure whether or not to move in with his girlfriend. *Man, Woman, Baby* took as its central thrust the dilemma faced by a thirty-something professional Londoner whose wife was expecting a baby that was missing a big toe. Crucially, though, they were all stories about uninteresting people with uninteresting lives uninterestingly told.

Despite this, there was little in the reams of increasingly vitriolic margin notes that Richard jotted that could implicate the books in SNAPS, nothing that Lauren could use to convince anyone that their theory needed to be acted upon. This was not going to be easy. Yet the more Richard read, the more determined he was to become a part of the process. Because this was books. And books really mattered.

Richard loved books. (Given the nature of independent bookselling – a vocation best suited to a minted eccentric or a congenital idiot – this was just as well.) True, for a spell, his head had been turned. For a year or so after he'd opened Back Street Books, happy in his relationship with Julie and determined to make a go of what he jokingly referred to as his career, he'd played the game. It had been a struggle – his eye for commercial fiction was somewhat jaundiced – but he'd tried to make sure that his esoteric fancies were balanced with a smattering of more commercially promising titles. He reasoned that if his customers wanted nothing more than the mundane, well, they could pay their money and they could take their choice.

But then Julie had left him.

From that moment, he'd done whatever was necessary to attack what they could have been to each other, what they might have meant had they stayed together. He'd breathed life into the future they would never know and he had given it a name. He had called it mediocrity.

There wasn't much he could do about Julie's relationship with the suburban norm. But his own? Well, that would change, goddammit. He would start with the obvious, and the books he sold. Then he would change the books he read. He would go back to the sort of stuff that had gripped him from the moment he *could* read, words that had left him tripping and shocked, teased and immersed in the banned, the dangerous, the blasphemous and transcendent, the grown-up and the plain and simply good. If mediocrity was standing still, the books he'd plug himself into would keep him on the move, jolt him into a new way of thinking and feeling and seeing, and every experiment, every formal twist or double-edged retrenchment, would underline for him the importance of spiking the mainstream, of rejecting convention, of subverting the mundane and doing things differently. And so he went back to William Faulkner and J.G. Ballard and Richard Brautigan. He reread Kerouac and Alasdair Gray, Samuel Beckett and Irvine Welsh, Virginia Woolf and Raymond Carver. He discovered Denis Cooper, Ron Butlin, Ann Quin, B.S. Johnson and Stewart Home. And as he read he was reminded that nothing had got his neurons sparking, nothing had made him come more thrillingly alive in the world, nothing had made him more attuned to the infinite shimmer of sentience or aghast at the heartlessness of understanding, nothing had made him feel more human than the words of writers like these.

And so. As Richard skimmed Gary Sayles, he felt himself grow full with renewed purpose. He knew there was mediocrity in all things, of course. In music and art and television and ideas and politics and love. But this was different. This was books. And when it came to books, you simply couldn't throw your hands up and allow yourself to accept the drift into the stew, the slide into the gloop. It was sacrilegious, wrong-headed, bottleless.

Because books mattered.

Books really mattered.

Late night phone call

Lauren mattered too. One night, after talking with him about his latest findings, she rang him again. It was an accident. Richard was sitting in front of his computer when he heard the phone go. He had been having trouble with his internet connection. He picked up and heard a click, some bleeps then another click. It was Lauren. She said, 'Oh, dammit...' and the line went quiet. Richard nearly blurted something calculatedly inappropriate, but he didn't. He stopped and listened, imagined her looking at her phone, deciding what to do. Considering her options. She pushed a button. There was another bleep but she had made a mistake, they were still connected. He pressed his handset to his ear. Listened harder. Heard unsilence. The sounds of the evening. His hard drive humming, a car in the street outside, someone banging the gate in the alley. A scratching from Lauren's house, the sound of a door closing. Footsteps, the rustle of paper.

He heard Lauren's body too. He heard her tut and sigh. He heard her move. He was sure he could hear her breathing. He sat like that for ten minutes. Just sat there. Listening to Lauren in the stillness. In the space between noises. Could almost feel her breathing, in time with his own... Finally, he hung up. Jesus, he thought, that was the world's strangest ever dirty phone call. Hot though. Very, very hot...

A *new impetus for Pippa and Zeke*

Pippa and Zeke are buying mannequins from shops that are closing down. A new project is at the point of conception. But Pippa's focus is not total. She is thinking about books. This doesn't happen very often. Books are like paint. They don't concern her much. But the third of their ongoing projects is book related. And it is sputtering into life.

Pippa and Zeke have discovered Gary Sayles. Posing as fans, they have set up and have maintained a Gary Sayles Facebook page, several Gary Sayles threads on various Kindle forums and an *I Love Gary Sayles* website. The website consists of extracts from his novels, snippets from interviews, made-up fan messages and a regularly updated list of *10 Things You Didn't Know about Gary Sayles*, five of which are invented. There are photographs, profiles of his fictional creations and a monthly quiz, the whole djinn bang.

Until two days ago, Pippa was unsure where the project would lead. Then two days ago Gary Sayles tweeted: 'wanted: my two biggest fans. drop me a line. together we can change the wolrd'. This seemed like an opportunity. Pippa responded.

'Remind me what the plan is?' says Zeke as they manhandle a dummy.

'Oh, I don't know,' says Pippa. 'Something head-less? Something with cocks?'

'Cocks and mannequins? Didn't someone do that in the nineties?'

'And? Cocks never go out of fashion, my dear. Speaking of, Gary Sayles got in touch. He'd like to meet us. To discuss an idea.'

'No. Really? How quaint! And I thought books were so oh-vah. Has he seen our work?'

'Apparently so.'

'The ten things?'

'Looks that way.'

'So spaghetti bolognese must *be* his favourite meal.'

'Must be.'

'And he must really like *The Vicar of Dibley*?'

'I reckon.'

'And his favourite film must *be A Wonderful Life*?'

'Didn't mention otherwise.'

'And his lifelong devotion to football must have started in 2002?'

'Darn tootin.'

'Strewth, that's some guesswork, right there, sister. A meeting, you say?'

'Yep.'

'When?'

'Next week.'

'Did he say what this idea was?'

'No. He was a little reticent.'

'But it will kick-start the project?'

'We'll see.'

'And what is the project again?'

'Oh, the usual,' says Pippa. 'Us. The world. A little

detachment, some punter projection. *Who we fuck and how we fuck 'em.* Is there anything else?'

'Biffo. Should we get dressed up?'

'Better had.'

'Can we film?'

'I should coco. After all. It's a multi-multi-meejah—'

'Extrav—'

'Or—'

'*Ganza!*'

'It is! It is! Zeke?'

'Pippa?'

'Shall we screw?'

'Churlish not to.'

Pippa and Zeke arrive home. Their flat is a carefully tended shambles, full of odds-and-sods and bits-and-bobs in which to stick the pins of inspiration. Pippa and Zeke raid their dressing-up drawer for next week's outfits, have sex. They lie on their bed, as they often do, pleased with themselves.

Later that day they choose their weapon. It is a VDR-D400 DVD video camera. They cut a hole in an Adidas holdall bag. They put the camera in the bag and test it. The camera films through the hole.

Truly these are exciting times for their art.

A wife is wary

'Mommy,' said Garfield Sayles one day, 'does Daddy write books?'

'Yes, love,' said Amy, 'Daddy writes books.'

'Does Daddy make up stories?'

'Sometimes, yes.'

'When Daddy makes up stories is he telling lies? Daddy said to me that making up stories was telling lies.'

'Yes, sometimes, sometimes it is.'

'But Daddy said that telling lies is bad. Mommy, is telling lies bad?'

'Most of the time,' said Amy. 'Most of the time telling lies is bad.'

Amy loved the conversations she had with her son. His curiosity glinted and shone. Whenever she talked with her husband they spoke about what they were going to watch on TV or what they had just eaten. Or how irony was like being knocked down by an ambulance. Or how the Internet Movie Database was much underrated as a tool of his trade. Or what they were going to do with the spare room. Or how the value of the house had fallen or risen. Sometimes he'd frown. His forehead would lower. Then the emphasis would change. He'd ask her how she *felt* about something. About what they had just eaten or what they were going to do with the spare room. Amy didn't resent this. It was necessary. It was part of the contract, part of being Man and Wife. She knew what she was involved in. It involved compromises. But although Amy told herself she was mostly content, she didn't draw much from these encounters.

With Garfield it was different. Each new reality was a star point of wonder, each conversation was an innocent interrogation of what she had come to rely on or turned to for release. Because of Garfield, she was looking closer at the story of her happy marriage.

The plot was just beginning to take on an unfamiliar aspect. The signs were there in the detail. Lately, Gary had been distant (although when she'd raised it with him, he'd suggested 'enigmatic'). Last week they hadn't made time to make love as he'd 'something on my mind'. Wednesday, she'd had to remind him to phone his mom. Just today, she'd been to their newsagent to find that he'd taken out a subscription to *Rural Property News*.

Amy was interested to see where Gary was going with this. She tolerated the life they shared. It had been what she was expecting. What she was ready for. It was an acceptable life for her, a good one for her son. But she wouldn't allow herself to become complacent. She was determined to keep on top of any sudden changes of direction in her family's story.

She talked it over several times with Garfield, in Garfield-speak. Just to keep her thinking fresh. Because whatever the significance of these details, Amy knew that Gary's use of 'enigmatic' was not a good sign.

Artists at work

That same day, Zeke and Pippa arrive at a café in Notting Hill for lunch. The venue is the choice of Gary Sayles. The café is full of people in PR. The chatter is loud, the faces are pale. Time moves busily, goes nowhere. The café serves breakfast and lunch with an American twist. Pippa is wearing a thin eggshell-blue cardigan from Next and a white market blouse. Black Gap jeans held up with a market white belt. A pair of Crocs Crocband mules. Enthusiastically applied Revlon Super Lustrous lipstick. White Musk. She flutters her eyelashes.

Zeke wears Lee jeans and Wrangler trainers, a Ben Sherman shirt and an FCUK baseball cap. They have both spent a lot of time on their hair. Pippa's is medium grilled, Zeke has a High Street number two. Pippa is carrying the bag.

Gary Sayles is sitting at a table in the window. He is wearing khaki chinos, loafers and a polo shirt. He has shades on his head. He doesn't look like an author. He looks like he has stepped from an advert for wine in a glossy Sunday magazine, above another for commemorative plates.

Holding a menu, he glances around the café. Every now and again he drops his chin on to his chest, buries his face into laminated breakfasts. His eyes peer over the top of the menu. He is hammy like a pig. It is as though he is anxious to be seen to be incognito. As

Zeke and Pippa approach his table he attracts the attention of a waitress.

'Hi. I'm Gary,' says Gary Sayles. Zeke and Pippa sit down. Pippa rests the bag on the floor, the camera focused on his crotch.

'And you must be...?'

'Susan,' says Pippa.

'Mike,' says Zeke.

'Hello?' says the waitress.

'Pleased to meet you,' says Gary.

'It's a privilege,' says Susan.

'An honour,' says Mike. 'We never thought we'd get the chance.'

'Oh, I don't know. I never forget the people who put me where I am.'

No one has acknowledged the waitress. She looks over her shoulder and then back to Gary. She says: 'Are you ready to order?' She has tired lines around bright blue eyes. Pippa has seen her somewhere before. She was at a party they threw a month ago. She is a friend of a friend. Pippa averts her gaze. Neither she nor Zeke can afford to be busted.

'Have what you want. It's on me,' Gary says, and waves a hand dismissively in the direction of the waitress. He speaks to Mike: 'I'm having an OJ.'

'Large or small?' the waitress asks Gary. She is still being ignored by Susan and Gary. She writes something on her pad. Mike thinks that by the look of her it isn't 'OJ'.

'Really?' says Susan, resolutely in character. 'That's good of you. I'll have a coffee, milk, one sugar. With some of that froth on top.'

'Tea for me,' says Mike. 'PG Tips if you've got it.'

The waitress nods and leaves. It is OK. Pippa and Zeke haven't been recognised. Gary sits up straight, brushes a hair off the sleeve of his shirt. He leans forward over the table.

'Thank you for coming,' he says. 'I'm glad you got in touch. I've been following your website for some time. You must be very dedicated.'

'Who wouldn't be?' says Mike.

'Indeed. Well, I'll not waste your time,' says Gary. 'I want to ask you a favour. I want to start a campaign and I want you – as my biggest fans – to be a part of it.'

'It would be an honour,' says Susan.

'What sort of a campaign?' says Mike.

'A campaign to reclaim literature,' says Gary. 'A campaign for the *democratisation* of literature.'

'The democratisation of literature?' says Susan.

Gary pauses. He is relaxing before them. He is speaking very slowly. He clearly has something important to say.

'Yes. I'll explain. You'll be aware that I'm a bestseller. Three times over. Well, I don't want to rest on my laurels. I want to change the face of books. I want to raise the profile of popular literature, to strike a blow for ordinary readers and what they read.'

'But how?' asks Susan.

'I have a new novel out soon. It's going to be called *The Grass is Greener*. It's about a thirty-five-year-old author who has a midlife crisis. He buys a sports car, has an affair and loses everything. You'll like it. Even if you haven't actually been there, it's all about recognition, it's all about familiarity. That's my gift.'

'Of course,' says Susan.

'You're a national treasure,' says Mike.

'That's very kind of you. My idea is to do with the promotion of the book. You may have seen things about how the internet is changing the way we live. Well I'll let you into a little secret: that's true of books too.

'Nowadays, when you bring a new book out, it's important that you do all you can to really connect with your readership. The old idea of the writer in the ivory tower, working away with a quill pen, has gone. Now it's all about being accessible. Showing your readers that you're really just like them.

'It used to be that you could do this by doing a reading tour. In bookshops, that sort of thing. But these days, everybody's doing readings. It's the internet that's done it. There are readings everywhere. People who aren't even published are reading their own stuff. It's making a mockery of the way you're supposed to bring a book to market.

'So I've come up with a little twist. No, please don't be alarmed! With *The Grass is Greener*, I want to take a back seat and let my readers represent me. I want to give readers the chance to read something from books that have been published. From my books. Mike, Susan, this is where you come in. On the next tour, I want you to read from my new book. I want you – the people – to take it to *the people*. Readings can be small, exclusive events. I want something more. I want to show what literature means to ordinary people, to the hundreds of thousands of ordinary people who buy my books. I was thinking about calling the tour the Fixed Rate Mortgage Tour...'

'What the fu—' says Pippa.

'It's got a ring to it,' says Mike.

'There's potential,' says Susan, 'definite potential.'

'But I've decided on the People's Literature Tour.'

'I see,' says Mike, 'like the People's Princess.'

'Aha,' says Gary, 'you see, I hadn't thought of that. But yes. Just exactly like the People's Princess. And let me tell you, the people will certainly be heard, let me assure you of that. This is just the beginning of it. I've got plans, big plans. So. Are you with me? Do you want to stand up for what you believe in? Shall we do this together? Will you take my book on the road?'

And Susan and Mike say: 'When do we start?'

They exchange details. Gary says he will be in touch. He leaves the café just as the waitress brings their drinks.

'It's OK,' says Pippa to the waitress, nodding her head at the retreating author, 'he's with us. We're on the case.'

'Yeah?' says the waitress. 'That figures.'

She walks away. Pippa shrugs. Turns to Zeke.

'So. Gary Sayles, author. Diss—'

'cuss,' says Zeke. 'Did we get it all on tape?'

'I think so.'

'And are you thinking what I'm thinking?'

'I am, I am.'

'He certainly has something, doesn't he?'

'And the rest.'

'"Everybody's doing readings because of the internet"?'

'It would appear so.'

'The People's Literature Tour?'

'You'd better believe it. All we need to do is keep filming—'

'Throw in a bit of the usual—'

'Ironic detachment—'

'Allusion to stuff—'

'And the punters'll love it. I can see it now. It'll be very clever and a little bit naughty. Either way we'll fuck him.'

'Fuck him good.'

'True dat. There's prizes for this sort of thing.'

'I see galleries...'

'A return to television...'

'The Turner...'

'Zeke? This could be the start of a beautiful friendship.'

A *wary wife writes*

Amy Sayles was beginning to wonder about her husband. About his stories.

She knew that everyone created stories. Everyone lived in parallel realities, make-believe worlds in which they were just a little bit bigger or happier or more organised or popular or successful or interesting or daring or normal than they were in their real lives. This was healthy. It was how people worked. It was how relationships worked. Men and women just far enough apart to be comfortable with each other's fictions. These stories became a threat only when they interfered with the lives of other people.

For much of their relationship, Amy had chosen to believe that Gary's stories were like his novels. Unthreatening. But she was beginning to wonder whether his personal fictions were more exotic than his novels let on.

It was unlikely. After all, he wasn't the most inventive of people. She knew that whenever he wrote about 'The One', he was writing about her. Whenever he wrote that a child was 'a bundle of joy with his daddy's ears', he was writing about Garfield. She remembered what had happened when he was working on his last book. He told Amy he'd run out of other people's experiences to gussie up his own with and had to resort to his imagination instead. He couldn't put anything down on paper for a week. Claimed it was writer's block.

Took to not shaving or getting dressed. Bought a box set of Guy Ritchie films (one of his 'guilty pleasures'). Commandeered Garfield's Lego, built a Death Star. He'd only come round after locking himself in his study for a whole day with a bottle of White's Lemonade, a six-pack of Golden Wonder Spicy Tomato Snaps and a copy of *The Best Ever Nineties Tunes Ever!* To get his 'mojo working again'.

But even so. There had been times when his fantasies had impinged on their life together. When he'd allowed himself to be diverted from what really mattered. In the lead-up to the publication of his second novel, for example. Gary had noticed that passages in the proof copy of the book bore no resemblance to what he'd originally written. Amy had tried to be diplomatic. Gary had been angry and precious. 'How dare they?' he'd said. 'Who do they think they're dealing with? I swear, if they're not careful, I'll go off-piste. Sign with someone else. There's plenty of people want a piece of Gary Sayles, I can tell you that for nothing.'

On that occasion, the digression had been harmless enough. Gary had stuck with his publisher, returned to the narrative they shared. This time Amy wondered whether he would.

Publishing phenomenon

Gary Sayles did his business at the printer's and set off home. He was late and had planned to take a cab but found himself instead at the nearest tube station. Standing on the deserted platform, he turned his collar up against the wind as it whistled noisily through the tunnel, reminding him of the Eurythmics song 'Here Comes the Rain Again' from the album *Touch*.

Gary had originally thought up the People's Literature Tour as a way of reaching more readers. After all, the name of the game was sales, and you couldn't afford to be complacent in this game, not with the internet getting involved. But since he had been exposed to the Ready Brek-like warmth of Mike and Susan's adulation, Gary had begun to believe his own press, or at least the press of the people who read his books. And now the idea had started to build up the momentum of a runaway lorry rolling full throttle down a hill with its handbrake off.

What was it that Mike had called him? A 'national treasure'? The People's Princess? At the time – and despite his distrust of false modesty – he'd let that go. But he was only speaking the truth. Was he not an icon? Was he not an outsider who was taking on an elitist establishment that had lost touch with popular opinion? It was funny to think of himself as an outsider, but it was what he was. There were plenty of people queuing up to criticise him, to poke fun at his brainpower. The critics for the national press. The people who wrote blogs dedicated to books that nobody read. The *bookish*. They were all running scared now, like the Iroquois Indians ran from Daniel Day-Lewis in *The Last of the Mohicans*, afraid he'd ruin their cosy little game. He knew that the secret to his success was that there was no secret. There were too many people with vested interests who made a big deal out of writing, when if you really wanted to make money out of it you just had to read books, see what everyone else was writing and then write the same.

Not that he was doing himself down, of course. He was unique, probably more unique than any of his rivals. The trick was to add just enough of your personality to what you were doing to make it stand out from the rest: he himself, for example, had been the first person ever to reminisce about 1980s synth bands.

It was this talent that had turned his very life around. Gary'd had it tough as a boy, growing up among people who thought he was a thicko and being kicked out of gangs by the 'tower block terrors'. He was too nerdy to be one of the boys and not mean enough to be one of the girls. It was only through his writing that he felt he'd really laid that ghost to rest. *Oh, he was nerdy all right. Nerdy like a fox!* On a trip back home to Birmingham, he'd seen a boy called Peter, who, in his schooldays, hadn't let Gary kick a ball because he hadn't helped to steal it from the sports shop. Peter drove a taxi now. Gary hadn't said anything. He'd just insisted Peter took a signed copy of his first novel by way of a tip. The taxi-driving former bully hadn't said anything in response. How could he? Gary had quite literally left him speechless.

The more he thought about his morning's encounter, the more Gary realised his relationship with his readers was the relationship that he had been looking for all his life. He loved Amy and Garfield, of course – his marriage certificate was proof enough of that – but writing was a great and exciting love, perhaps *the* great and exciting love. For too long he'd thought that he'd be nothing without the people. Now he could see that the people would be nothing without him.

As he stood on the platform, fresh from his meeting with the besotted Mike and the lovely Susan, this love washed over him like a tidal wave. It was unconditional, like water, yet it filled him with a sense of responsibility, as though he were a lifeguard on the beach of life. It provided him with the fulfilment of Gary Sayles, the man himself, that he had looked for for so long. So this, *this was what it meant to be a writer!*

The train arrived and Gary found himself a seat in a carriage. This was apt. Journeys, life was all about journeys, he could see that now. Where would he go from here? His thoughts drifted like crisp white snow. He would hitch his wagon to a rising star – his own – and see.

And how!

Underestimated

Gary presented the T-shirts to Amy with a flourish. They were thick cotton and coloured in a variety of funky shades. The front of each was printed with the heads of Gary, Amy and Garfield. They had been taken from a family portrait they'd had done the year before. Amy and Garfield were in the foreground with Gary behind them. Amy couldn't be sure but at first glance it was almost as if Gary's head was slightly out of proportion.

'What do you think, then, Angel Cakes?' asked Gary.

Amy was sitting reading to Garfield on the sofa. All week Gary had been shutting himself off in his study. Keeping most unsociable hours. Garfield had begun to ask questions. Amy had answered him truthfully. She had defended Gary's right to take himself away. But that was as far as she would go. Now she had questions for her husband.

'I don't know. I'm not sure. What are they for?'

Gary flipped a T-shirt over. On the back, Amy read:

GARY SAYLES

PRESENTS

THE PEOPLE'S LITERATURE

'I don't understand,' she said.

'They're promotional shirts for the launch of *The*

Grass is Greener. It's time for Gary Sayles to get the credit he deserves.'

Amy looked at Gary. She had read the odd page of *The Grass is Greener*, of course. She'd read parts of all of his books as they were being written, with Gary pointing out wordplays and the occasional pun. The latest wasn't to Amy's taste but – the age of the protagonists aside – it was not significantly different to any of the others he had written. So why was he introducing T-shirts now? And why was he talking to her as if she were an idiot? She picked up Garfield, hefted him on to her lap. Claimed him.

'OK. But why am I on there? And Garfield? And what's the People's Literature?'

'I'm spreading the word,' said Gary, 'just spreading the word. You see, Amy, literature isn't just about telling stories. It's about creating other people's lives for them on and off the page. Giving them something to look up to, showing them the way. This is the responsibility I have to my readers. Do you know, I met two people the other day, two of my biggest fans? A couple of ordinary people. And they put a few things into perspective for me. What I mean to them, to my readers. I hadn't realised before, not quite. They didn't say much, these two. They were tongue-tied. I see now that this is how my readers must feel all the time. Inarticulate. They look around and they struggle to make sense of the world. They need a voice. They need to be heard. So they turn to me because they know that whatever else may go on, Gary Sayles will keep writing novels that will give them their voice.'

'But...'

'Wait. This is important. The funny thing is, all these years I've been working towards this moment. I've got everything I've always wanted. I'm successful. I'm married to a lovely lady. I've got a beautiful son. And now I'm there, I've realised it's only the beginning. That's what the People's Literature Tour is all about. Amy, I think I've found my destiny.'

'OK. So what are you going to do? With this whole T-shirt thing?'

'Oh, all sorts. Big things. I'm working on things.'

As Gary said this, he reached out and lightly touched the top of her head. Smoothed her hair. The contact was gentle. It was the first they'd had for some time. It was the old Gary. Amy felt his hand there again and then again. She flinched.

'The point is, I can do anything. Don't you see? I am the voice of hundreds of thousands of people. They come to me and I put their lives into words, make sense of their lives for them. Amy, *I can do anything.*'

Gary's voice was tight with a thrill that Amy had not heard before. He was breathing heavily. His pupils were dilated. In his profile there was something Amy hadn't seen before. Something about the upward tilt of his chin.

'I think we need to talk,' said Amy. 'I know you've got work to do but I think we need to talk. Come and sit down.'

'Not just now, My Little Pretty One. Things to do. If you want me I'll be upstairs in my study.'

And with that he left the room. Amy frowned. She was used to being underestimated. It never really bothered her. Let other people think what they wanted. It was their mistake. But My Little Pretty One? Angel Cakes? *Gary Sayles?* Gary Sayles had just patted her on the head. And Gary Sayles should know better.

Amy

Amy had her own stories, of course. Stories about marriage and family. Everyday stories.

Growing up, her family had been a mess. She was twelve when her mom left her dad. It was autumn. The wind was gusty and Amy arrived home late from school with leaves in her hair. Her dad sat in the kitchen, looking at where the tiles met the bare plaster on the wall. Her mom had just taken a bag of clothes and disappeared. She'd left one note for Amy and one for her dad. To Amy she wrote: 'I'll always be there for you' and 'there's more to life than playing at happy families'.

Even without the shepherd's pie drying in the oven, it was a clichéd affair. Amy's dad couldn't understand it. He'd always been a good husband. Didn't she remember the special trips he would make to the kitchenware shop for Christmas and her birthday? He'd been generous to a fault. Pans, serving bowls, place mats. One year a plastic pinny with a cow on the front. They'd had a routine. Her: cooking, washing up, hoovering and shopping. Him: grouting the bathroom, cutting the hedge, brewing his own beer. Sundays they'd sit down to eat together in front of the TV. Every two months they went out to their favourite restaurant. Each year there'd be the same holiday, to their caravan in Rhyl. They liked it there. These were the things that mattered. It didn't bother them that there were sometimes rows. Or that the two of them didn't always see eye to eye. Or even that his routine differed slightly from hers. He was a self-employed builder. She ran the house and worked part-time in a bakery. It was bound to happen. A lot of the time he was out doing business. Making contacts with friends and people in the trade, 'putting the word around'. Amy and her mom were lucky that most of his contacts drank in his local and they saw as much of him as they did.

They still had time together. Amy remembered, didn't she? When he was home in the evenings he'd stay up late in front of the TV. Working on his paperwork, sampling his homebrew. She'd often stay up with him. He'd crack jokes. Did she remember the one about the flasher and the nun? He was funny and she loved him. Didn't she? It wasn't his fault her mom wasn't always able to stay up. She was too tired a lot of the time. And she was often crabby in the evenings anyway. Now Amy must have remembered that?

They had each other and they had their routine. And he'd never looked at another woman the whole time they'd been married. What else could he have done?

It was obvious her mom was in denial, he said. She'd been on the phone. She'd told him she was happy in her new life. She'd started night school and dance classes. Her friends spoke of new men; a dough-maker, a teacher, possibly a Spaniard. She'd started going to different restaurants, some of which he knew she wouldn't like. He just didn't know what to make of it all.

Amy did. When her mom had got back in touch with her, she had tried to act as peacemaker. But her dad was missing the point. It wasn't just about him. His lack of imagination – before or after the split – affected them all. And even though she loved him, she pitied his *wheeee!*-ing slide into self-pity.

He began to drink more and work less. When he was drunk he would complain about being depressed. He would spend hours in front of the television, just whomping, whomping between channels with an all-in-one TV and video remote.

And then there were the books. Her dad had started reading, going through the paperbacks on the small shelf in the kitchen. Thrillers. Adventure stories. Comfort reads. But Amy knew this was the wrong sort of comfort. It was this sort of comfort that had got them to where they were now, that had left him sitting in his armchair, sliding heavy-lidded into a slough of Wilbur Smith-ed despond. Exasperated, Amy encouraged him to get up earlier in the morning. To get out of the house more, to look for work. To stop moping. She offered to pay him to leave the house whenever she had boys round; she thought she could tease him into change. It was no good. He wouldn't be told.

It was frustrating bringing up her dad. But Amy was an adaptable girl. She grew up very quickly. And she realised that there were more useful ways to spend her future than pitty-pattying around men until the story of her life had been written for her. She would use her imagination. She would take control.

Unlike, it seemed, her peers. When she arrived at university, she had been disappointed to meet her fellow female students. They were mostly a clueless, soft-thinking bunch, happy to have their lives written for them, to follow the path of least resistance through the world.

It was 2001 and the fashion was for ladettes or women who simpered. Sexual politics were passé: the multi-stranded narrative of men and women had been reduced once more to the story of Boy meets Girl. Most of those who simpered did so under the illusion they were simpering ironically, from a position of strength. But it was not an edifying sight. And whichever way you tried to skirt the issue, Ms was Miss once more. Now *there* was a lack of imagination. It was not for Amy. Her mom had taught her better than this.

Her first lesson had been that you couldn't put a price on financial independence. Amy had absorbed this. Two months into her first year, so skint that she was eating own-brand stuffing on toast, she had responded to an ad in the *Warwick Student*. It offered the opportunity to 'Earn While U Learn' and led her weekly to Birmingham; for two nights a week she was paid cash for a range of services from hand jobs to full sexual intercourse.

Amy was pragmatic about the business. Although the men were pigs, the money was good. And the men would be pigs with or without her financial remuneration. It was as simple as that.

Not that everyone saw it this way. There were some who thought that sex workers were making a statement. About attitudes to prostitution. About feminism. About post-feminism. Amy knew better.

It was true that in the approach to the new millennium, under the muffling cover of generic cultural hysteria, a quiet shift had taken place. Strip clubs were now 'respectable', table dancing 'acceptable'. Selling yourself was 'empowering'. But although Amy was in a transparently honest and comparatively well-paid job, she didn't feel 'empowered' by her work. And she didn't know anyone else who did either.

As the weeks scurried day by day into months it was unavoidable that Amy's opinion of men would narrow. The clowns she came into contact with were even worse than her dad. They were such an undignified lot, all gesture, wife-love and grunt. Those that hadn't the wit to take advantage of being men had the front to bleat about their lot. Insistently, as though *they* bore the troubles of the world.

Then there were the haters and their angry fucking and their uninspired variations on the inevitable line about 'loving women too much'. Again, it was the lack of imagination that Amy couldn't fathom. Could they not open their eyes? Look around and present the world with something a little different? Where was their pride?

A couple of months into her third year, she quit the game. Stopping work was no more of an issue than starting it – she was just knackered. And her need to concentrate on her studies was now a more pressing concern than the content of her high-interest savings account. Shortly afterwards, she got a job at the Warwick Arts Centre. It wasn't so bad. She had a presence behind the bar. Tips were good. She was asked out by lots of men. She said no to them all.

Until she met Gary again. Gary was not like the other men she'd known. He was no dazzler but he was no arsehole either. He was honest. Dependable. Kind. Enthusiastic. Genuinely solicitous of her needs. And although he liked routine, he wasn't the sort to stick in a rut. He was too driven for that, had always shown too much gumption. Amy could see him as a father.

Three months after they met each other in the bar, Gary had presented Amy with an H Samuel ring. He talked of dreams come true. They were married a week after her graduation. Amy wore white. The reception was held in the function room of a functional hotel on the Bristol Road. It passed in a droll frenzy of vol-au-vents and taxis and bone-diseased aunts. In his speech, Gary called it a 'seventeen-year whirlwind romance'. It was a line of Amy's.

Five conventionally happy years later, she gave birth to their son, Garfield. Amy had always wanted kids and she was especially happy when she had a son. Amy wanted Garfield to be different from other men. She wanted him to know more than other men about what it meant to be a man. She would share with him her stories and what she had learned from her life and she would show him how he could be different from the men she had known.

A short story by Richard, a setback for Lauren

Three days after they had met at her house, Lauren opened her email at work to find she had a message from Richard:

Dear Lauren,

So this is a thought that occurred to me at your house the other day. It may have been the Merlot that got me thinking – or the Cab Sauv or the Shiraz – but I decided to share it with you anyway, as – you never know – you might find it comes in handy at some point.

I saw your books, you see. And all I saw was fol-de-ra and ra-dee-yay and nice little portraits of worlds decorated by the dead white scholars of Decorum Inc. The thing is, books should be more than this. It's a writer's job to stimulate. To *provoke*. To prod and poke people into wanting more, not to cop out. Not to paper over the cracks in the wall.

And we should encourage them too. We should read the good stuff. Because let's face it, wanting more is all there is. We should all want more than just existence, more than just our neurons sparking or reflexes reflexing. More than mediocrity. We should want to live life. And if we're going to live life we have to grab it by the throat and throttle it up and out from inside, and whether or not we can – whether or not we do – is down to the books we read, the art we look at, the music we listen to. We're all affected by all of this, all of the time. It matters.

You might think that this is another one of my 'abstract' ideas, another little point in a 'theoretical debate'. But it isn't. In fact I'd go so far as to say that no one can begin to fully understand SNAPS without grasping this.

Any road. I don't think you've read any of my stuff yet. So I thought I'd send you this story, by way of illustration.

Respectfully yours, lots of love, etc. etc.

Mr Richard Anger Esq, 'The Attic', Harborne

Lauren felt herself flush. She took a deep breath. At first she thought she might have missed something. It certainly seemed that way. Taken at face value, what the message lacked in presumption – and it did presume a great deal – it made up for with its condescending style. Yet although she found it easy to believe that Richard could be presumptuous he was certainly in no position to condescend to her. Perhaps he was making a point about Lauren working harder as a reader. Perhaps the mail was merely a satirical companion piece to his story; when she read the attachment, maybe it would become clear. She opened the file and began to read.

It was called 'Untitled'. It was the tale of an angry bookshop owner who drank himself out of business and into an underground society of murderous anarcho-booksellers. The story was gruesome. It was bathetic. It was polemical, uncoordinated, chaotic...

Lowrie sat in the corner of the room, her limbs were bound in leather. Her mouth was shut fierce and her shirt gapped open, skin freckling to distant nipples. They could be a team. He saw that. They could work together. But first he had to slip her the words.

The worlds within words.

There were worlds within words and Rick was ready to slip them to Lowrie and then he was ready to twist the world on its axis, to show Lowrie more clearly the sun.

$$Be$$

$$words$$

$$cause$$

$$twist$$

$$the\ world.$$

He had them all. She would see. And then she would see that the world as it was, without his words, was cnuts.

THE WORLD

IS CNUTS.

He'd words he'd picked up first-hand (or second-hand, barely thumbed). These he'd slip her and then when she was eye-scorched by the light, while she was away and musing on their worlds, he'd tell her, his muse, I've had it with gaping at your gapping, I want to play before we kill, then they'd get down to it and after 10 minutes of clock-watched

crotch scraping Rick would have spurted, splurted
(phlegmy, furtive)

Christ I need a drink…

Lauren knew what he meant. She had hoped that Richard's understanding of books and of writing would advance their investigations into SNAPS. But although she wasn't as widely read as he was, she was sure of one thing: writing was about reaching out to other people, whatever you wanted to say. Whether your intention was to move people or to move them along, you had first to connect, to make connections. She could see he had a point about reaching too far, about handing people things on a plate. But there was a difference between 'copping out' and ranting angrily in an underground of your imagination. Self-absorption wasn't the answer. If anyone knew that, Lauren did. And Richard's writing connected with nothing. Certainly not to her, as a reader or a person.

Her annoyance was compounded by a sense of disappointment. True, she remained wary of Richard. In the short time she'd known him, he'd been infuriating, needy and almost permanently drunk and obnoxious. Lascivious too. She had pretended not to notice, but when they had met at her house he had proposed a tryst, an idea as perplexing as it was absurd. He clearly had myriad faults. Yet there was something about the chemicals in his brain and the patterns they formed, something about the neurological grammar and synaptic elisions of the language of his mind, that intrigued as much as it appalled. He was – in simple terms – making her life more interesting. It had been a long time since she had discussed with anyone matters that weren't related to work or landscape photography, or any of the other hobbies she'd embraced in order to fill long holiday hours in places without Will. And despite the challenges he presented, Lauren had even begun to consider the possibility that a friendship might develop between them.

Well, it wasn't going to if he carried on like this. So far she had tolerated his provocations, maybe even subconsciously indulged them. After all, that was the point of her experiment. But this time he was asking too much. There was nothing she could take from this story. She couldn't even tell what – if anything – he was trying to give. It read as a gesture of pure indulgence.

In one respect, however, she was forced to concede that he had proved himself. By no stretch of the imagination was *Untitled* mediocre.

It was bloody awful.

Dear Richard,

I read your story. I have to say I am unconvinced of its merits. Having said that, I fear your distinction between good and bad readers may apply in this instance. Certainly, if my reaction to it is one of the criteria by which you make the judgement, then I concede that I may fall into the latter camp.

With regard to our evening, I'm pleased to hear that you took it upon yourself to undertake a critical appraisal of my reading habits, unencumbered as you were by any idea of what they may be. For your information I don't read too much at the moment.

I haven't for a while. People say they like the order it brings to things. For some time now my work and my photography have taken care of that particular need. There has been much beyond this that I have had no need to make sense of.

As for SNAPS, I will admit that the points you made about the relationship between reading and life were interesting, if not wholly original. I have recently been giving this very matter some careful thought. I have no doubt that 'books can change you'. I also think there is something to be said for indulging yourself in the work of those who would imagine different ways of living; I wouldn't be a scientist if I didn't acknowledge this.

However, I am equally unsure that this is 'all there is'. Maybe you will be able to enlighten me on this matter one day. Maybe even without the benefit of alcohol. It would be nice to think so.

Lauren

Lauren advances

After sending her reply, Lauren spent the rest of the afternoon trying to stop herself from brooding. She made cups of lemon and ginger tea, toyed with the bags until the water cooled to tepid. Browsed a journal, read a paper on the link between right-hemisphere trauma and borderline personality disorder. She even essayed a stab at a half-remembered t'ai chi exercise in an effort to ease the tension in her neck. It was no use. Whether he was demonstrating a neural anomaly or decrying the importance of deep breathing, Richard was there at the edge of her consciousness, provoking her.

By the end of the afternoon she found herself looking out of the window of her office. Here, at least, was respite from the world in the view of the slowly changing season as it percolated across the quad. Today the canopy of the sycamore was resplendent in caterpillar green, doily-edged with ochre and lemon. The shadows on the brickwork opposite were fluid, the late summer light growing more brilliant and involved with every passing minute.

She found her eyes drawn to a couple of students, a boy and a girl. They looked very young. Lauren supposed they were a particular type of young, but she had no idea which it might be. They were sitting close together on the grass, under the tree. They were looking at each other intently, the soles of their feet touching. The scene played out in unreal primary colours, the yellows and reds of their clothes heightened in the sunlight against the verdant depth of the grass. The boy leaned forward and muttered something into the girl's ear. At first Lauren thought this might have been a joke, or an imaginative hypothesis. But then the girl recoiled exaggeratedly and Lauren saw the indignation on her face.

A moment later she was standing up, squashing her feet into her pumps and stomping away like a Mediterranean child, pausing only to turn to her rising companion and offer him her middle finger, theatrically and without compunction. The hapless boy sat still, his palms facing the sky as she walked away.

Lauren thought again of the cause of her disquiet. Richard's story had been crass and casual to the point of unfeeling. Yet maybe she had been too hasty in taking offence. Her decision to let go of Will and all that he had come to mean hadn't been taken lightly, and she intended to honour the seriousness of its intent. It was all very well exposing herself to the possibilities of a new way of living but she had to be able to relax into them. Richard had whispered obscenities in her ear. But that was Richard, that was what Richard did. Lauren didn't have to react in the way she had, she didn't need to retreat into herself. There was another way.

The girl's gesture in the quad was both vulgar and antisocial. But there was something liberating about the attitude it represented. It was careless, unrestrained. It looked like fun. Lauren remembered fun. She used to eat at country pubs, she'd once spent an afternoon at the cinema watching – now what was his name again? – Jacques Tati. That had been fun. Well, sort of, anyway. There'd been lots of non-Will-related things too. She'd been on a barge one summer, a long time ago, just after her A levels; as a child she'd played hide-and-seek with the daughter of her cello teacher, giggling behind a yellow bush in their back garden near Sutton Park, while her mother discussed gradings and chords...

Lauren sat back down at her desk and rested her arm on its elbow. She clenched and unclenched her fist, looked at the veins, the joints, the tendons moving beneath the skin. Then she practised extending the middle finger and offering it, slowly and deliberately, to the door and to the walls of her office, to the world outside her window, and to the annoyingly significant Richard too.

In which Lauren accepts the value of Richard's way of working

One evening, Richard emailed Lauren a story from that day's *Bookseller*:

> Barker Follinge are sad to announce the death of Katie Roberts. Katie, 39, who recently moved to the editorial team following five years in the marketing department, died suddenly at her home on Tuesday. An inquest will be held into her death.
>
> The tragedy is the second to befall the BF editorial team in the run-up to the publication of the imprint's lead autumn title. In May, Elizabeth Menzies, a BF editor, died of a brain condition.

Lauren was appalled but excited too. This was a significant development. She rang Richard.

'I think we should change our approach,' she told him. 'I had hoped to have discovered some evidence for the connection between SNAPS and these books by now, but I haven't. And too many people are dying for us to wait any longer. So, although all that we have to work with is anecdotal, I suggest we proceed on the assumption that there is a causal link. What is important now is that we get the message out: these books kill.'

'Blimey,' said Richard. 'You've changed your tune, haven't you?'

'It's just something about this story. It's made me reconsider what we saw in Corfu. When Elizabeth Menzies died, she was reading the manuscript of Gary Sayles' new novel—'

'Yeah. The poor cu—'

'And there was nothing to suggest she'd just read any of his earlier work. Similarly, there's no good reason for his present editor – this Katie Roberts – to be going over his first three novels. Just as there is no evidence that the consular official who died had read more than one of his books. Which means that although we once thought SNAPS may have been caused by sustained exposure to Sayles' novels, it may well be that just one will kill. Maybe... maybe even part of one.'

'Blimey.'

'Indeed. I mean, is there a chance, could it be possible, that his books are actually getting worse?'

'Having read the first three I have to say it's very unlikely,' said Richard. 'But either way, I see what you mean about getting on with it. Because if you're right, in about six weeks' time more people are going to die.'

An artist prepares to clinch the deal

That afternoon, Pippa and Zeke are sitting up on their bed smoking pipes. Zeke is fully clothed. Pippa is naked. She is playing a game called Whatever Happens with Mary Jane where she smokes Manali until she is full and then masturbates with Wet Original Classic Gel.

Zeke rubs his eyes. He is trying to clear his mind. Pippa's brain is crazy-paved. They have been talking about their art. Pippa has grown tired of the *Evening Post* obituary verse project. It is taking too long. It is difficult to see who will buy into it and how. Now she is looking for replacement revenue streams. Last week she placed an ad in the smalls of *Time Out* and the listing mags of Chester, Birmingham, Grimsby and Bath. It said: 'Artists for Hire. Nothing Considered. Flash Mobs and Spectacles for the Non-Discerning Punter.'

'What the fuck?' asked Zeke.

'Nothing Considered? It's an encapsulation of our modus operandi,' Pippa explained. 'And the rest? Catchy, huh?'

'Hmm,' said Zeke.

Now Pippa is obsessing about Gary Sayles. The project's potential, she says, is unlimited. Zeke is not convinced.

'Isn't it, you know, a bit out there?'

'C'mon, Zeke, break a leg. You're forgetting. All we are is who we fuck and how we fuck 'em. There ain't nothing else. This is us, this is our art. You know that.'

'Yeah, but can't you just slow down a bit?' says Zeke. 'I'm not feeling at the top of my game at the moment. I don't want to waste my energy.'

'I didn't notice you had any energy to waste,' says Pippa.

Zeke and Pippa have not had sex in three days. Pippa wants sex. Without sex, Zeke knows that Pippa is fractious, bolshy.

She sings, 'Verily mine knickers doth smoulder and oh, how I long for your hose.'

Clearly she is spoiling for a fight. When they fight, Pippa and Zeke fight like family. Like lovers on the high street of a market town. But Zeke is not in the mood for a fight tonight. Zeke is tired. Zeke has been tired for three days. It is the books making him tired. He has been reading a volume of Gary Sayles' first three books at night, so he will know how to play Mike when he is up on stage as part of the People's Literature Tour. The books are alien to him. It is as though he is reading science fiction. Surely no one actually lives like this? Still, they exert a strange pull. Still, he turns the pages.

Zeke is unsure where the Sayles Project might lead. But Pippa knows. That is why she is overexcited. Throughout their career, their art has meant nothing. It has been empty of meaning. Throughout their career, punters have paid to make of it what they will. They have crammed it full of their own stuff. Pippa and Zeke have been called post-Duchamp, post-Warhol, post-Ono. They have been claimed by the disciples of Dada, Surrealism, Situationism, Fluxus. But they have believed in none of these things.

Now it is time to fess up. To spill the jumping beans, to produce the great reveal. To demonstrate to punters and critics alike that Pippa and Zeke have played them like kazoos. To show them that Art Means Nothing, or even less than that.

For what is the point of taking the piss if no one sees the piss is being taken? Of being clever if no one can see how clever you are?

The film of the People's Literature Tour is the perfect vehicle for their revelation. The author is an idiot. He takes his work so gosh darn seriously that the story will tell itself. The footage of Zeke as Mike will be intercut with a montage of Zeke and Pippa's finest moments. There will be sex, violence, comedy dwarves. Some of the soundtrack will be their mocking laughter. Some of it will be telephone conversations recorded on an average Tuesday, about box sets of the Californian beat combo Bongwater and pornographic imagery on the information superhighway.

Pippa has the opening shots of the film in her head:

> Gary Sayles in the café.

> Soundtrack: 'I want you – the people – to take it to the people.'

> Cut to Mike looking gormless, Mike-like, at a copy of *Cutting the Cake*.

> Cut to Zeke. Zeke frowns.

Soundtrack: 'Who is your god?' <Check source.>

Cut to Zeke a month before.

Zeke wears a blond pig-tailed wig. It bounces. He is scrawny and diabolical-looking. He is fucking that simpering big-titted student to some tune from *Don Giovanni* and chugging from a bottle of peachy schnapps.

Cut to Sayles: 'ordinary people with ordinary problems'.

Repeat to fade.

The resulting masterpiece will be the ultimate anti-art statement. It will destroy the idea of meaning in art. It will destroy the idea of art itself.

Pippa knows and Pippa believes. All she needs is to arrange one more piece of footage to complete the film. Something to illustrate the po-mo credo. Something to show what Zeke and Pippa have done to art. *Who we fuck and how we fuck 'em.* Indeed. It will be shown as the closing credits roll.

She rolls over, exhales deeply, picks up a pen from the side of the bed. Writes the note on a piece of writing paper. The paper has flowers in the top right corner. It is cerise. She bought it from Clintons. She sprays it with White Musk and puts it in an envelope.

As he lies on his back next to Pippa, Zeke closes his eyes and feels himself sweat. The room is hot and full of smoke. Zeke is feeling the pressure, unsure of his role in the Sayles Project. He does not have long to get himself prepared. This evening he and Pippa are going round to the author's house for a meeting about the launch of the People's Literature Tour. Gary has told them that the first reading is in just four weeks' time.

Next to him, on the bed, Zeke hears a familiar click followed by a hum. Then Pippa humming. It is Charlotte Charles. Now Pippa is just being bloody-minded. Wilful. It is not Zeke's fault he has been unable to perform. All the reading has given him aches in his head.

In which Richard is running out of ideas...

Richard was struggling. The more he tried to put a boot up the arse of his relationship with Lauren, the tighter she seemed to clench. She just didn't seem prepared to take a chance on a life-changing liaison with a bloke as challenging as he was.

This reticence didn't just wind Richard up, it worried him too. He couldn't expect everyone to embrace the deviant with quite the elan that he did, but neither was it healthy to remain so uptight. Even though Lauren wasn't by any stretch of the most delirious imagination a devotee of the mediocre, the poor woman was in danger of only living half a life.

He'd thought his story might help. *Untitled* was thickly rich, daringly personal and – to the right sort of reader – deeply rewarding. He'd spent a whole week on rewriting and revision, a long time for Richard to work on a story. He had written it specifically for Lauren, to show her the potential in transgressive fiction and a life less 9–5. With the accompanying email he'd even introduced an element of playful abuse into the exchange. (This had been bold. As he was writing, he'd made a severe dent in a bottle of Count Orloff vodka, an inexpensive and not entirely authentic brew that had its origins in a factory centre just outside Rowley Regis. And the combination of the

Count and playful abuse had been under-appreciated before.)

At the very least he'd expected the correspondence to have shocked Lauren into an emotional outburst. So how had she reacted? She'd bunted him. Jesus, she'd bunted him. He'd written some put-downs in his time – to editors who'd rejected his innovative prose and didn't see themselves for the industry whores they were – but none had been more off-handedly devastating than Lauren's.

Had his maverick tendencies and incorrigible wit simply been too much for her? For a moment he almost convinced himself they might have been. But no. The truth was less exotic than that. The difficulty was that this kind of thing alone was not going to be enough to woo a woman like the Prof.

Richard knew he had to tailor his approach, to find a more Lauren-friendly way of attracting her attention. Something that would show her another side to his personality, introduce her to the boiling cauldron of contradictions that was Richard Anger.

He began by looking for ideas in the half-remembered snippets of their last proper conversation. Lauren had claimed his knowledge was 'abstract', she'd mentioned the need for 'objective analysis'. She'd questioned whether he was 'adequately informed'. It was obvious what she wanted there: a methodical, reasoned approach, softly softly bores the monkey. Irksome though this was, it was doable. All he had to do was wind his neck in, cut down on the expletives, deaden his chat with a few facts and figures. But while this was a necessary expediency, it was also a bit pissy, less boiling cauldron than simmering milk pan. If he was going to go all number-cruncher on the woman, he needed something else, something that would make an equally effective impression on her without compromising his devotion to the extreme.

He thought on. 'Why do you drink so much?' Lauren had asked and then, her lips pursed like a kitten's arse, 'I see.' In her email she had also made a sniffy reference to his alcohol consumption. Maybe there was something there? Richard mulled, projected and mulled some more. And then it came to him, like the smash of an own-brand supermarket whisky: for his next trick, Richard was going to be sober.

The idea was perfect. Lauren might have reserve to spare but not even she could fail to be moved by the audacity of a gesture like that. Richard Anger? *Sober?* Why, it would knock the woman bandy!

Sure, it was a controversial step. Richard liked drinking too much. It was the behaviour of the outcast and the rebel, the writer's vice. There was a tradition of noble sots and visionary lushes, romantics, expressionists, Beats, experimenters all. Yet Lauren, infuriatingly, had a point. There was another side to being a drunk. Richard was uncomfortably aware that his habit was sometimes less about provoking a response than being stuck in a rut of sloshing liquor. And that way, he knew, lay mediocrity; that way lay atrophy and a social SNAPS.

Whichever way you cut it, the idea was on the bingo. He would embrace sobriety, demonstrate to her his flair for the contrary, and finally – *finally* – convince her of his credentials as an anti-heroic lover...

That was the theory anyway. In practice, Richard was struggling. The three days he'd been alcohol free had shown him how convincing he could hope to be as an abstainer. Not very. In daylight hours he had been given a taste of what to expect if he was regularly exposed to the obscene clarity that accompanied his sober state. Several times he'd nearly gone under and reached for the bottle of medicinal hooch he kept behind the till.

Once he'd had an exchange with a student who'd wandered in out of the rain.

'Have you got a copy of the *Lonely Planet Guide to South East Asia on a Shoestring*?'

'No, I don't sell guidebooks. There's an Oxfam bookshop at the top of the hill. You could try them.'

'You're joking, aren't you? I'm not going all the way up there.'

On a more thirst-making occasion still, he'd dismantled a display of dissident Chinese fiction to discover that he'd sold not a single copy, not of Gao Xingjian nor Yiyun Li nor Liao Yiwu nor Ma Jian. It was almost as if nobody cared.

And then there were the nights. At night he'd lain in bed, sweating fear. Whereas SNAPS had once seemed to offer him a shot at salvation – professionally at least – now the resonance of bodies hitting stone floors and lives abruptly interrupted began to torment him. He'd felt the drumming insistence of sleeplessness and dreamed hallucinatory and wakeful dreams. He'd seen stars and looked at far-flung lights and feared the shadows in the corners of his room. And he'd found himself asking the question, over and over again. What would he leave behind if he were to be struck down the very next day by a brain disorder? A virtual sheaf of unpublished masterworks? Or of transgressive embarrassment?

Richard knew that he couldn't go on like this. He was crazed through lack of sleep. He needed to see Lauren and soon, to share with her this latest manifestation of his nonconformist creed. He needed to show her that he was ready to confront a terrible personal truth and move on.

Then he could have another drink...

Richard is sober, Lauren has some fun

Richard and Lauren caught up next in the Shakespeare in Birmingham city centre. Meeting in a pub wasn't the temporarily sober Richard's idea of a genius plan – he'd suggested Lauren's place – but Lauren seemed unaccountably keen.

Richard arrived early and bagged a table in the corner furthest away from the bar. He covered it with visual aids: a ring-bound notepad, a couple of glossy trade mags and pages of figures and pie charts. None of them was relevant to SNAPS, but that didn't matter. Lauren wouldn't be getting closer to them than he needed her to.

So:

Impressive-looking paperwork?

Check.

Head full of restraint?

Check.

Lime and soda?

Check.

The scene was set.

When Lauren arrived, Richard stood and gestured to the chair opposite. Then he sat back down and frowned intently at one of his printouts, a table of children's audiobook sales he'd photocopied from the *Bookseller*.

'Good evening Lauren,' he said, without looking up. 'Before we start, I thought it might be instructive if we had a little recap of the situation to date. Now, my understanding is that at the moment we haven't sufficient evidence of the damaging effects of Sayles' books to formally present our case to any of the parties who may be able to provide us with assistance. Would you say that's a fair assessment?'

'Gosh,' said Lauren. 'I mean, I think so.'

'Good,' said Richard as he underlined something in his notebook, 'and so to business. And what we *can* do. The first thing is to speak to a few newspaper people. If we can get them to carry even a small news story about a possible link between Gary Sayles and SNAPS, it'll be a start. But we need to move quickly. His latest shit-smearing is due out in about five weeks but by then it will already have been read quite widely: reviewers and booksellers will get their copies long before it's due to hit the shelves. So we're looking at the first finished books being in circulation in about, ooh, a week. If they're not already.'

Richard caught himself. It was a good start – sober and apposite – but then 'shit-smearing' had somehow slipped out. Had she noticed? He didn't think so but he'd have to be careful.

'Either way,' he continued, 'to give you an idea of what we're up against if we don't give ourselves enough time to put the mockers on – to arrest the *momentum* of the book's publicity campaign – I have some data for you.'

And he had too. Minute after minute of statistics,

each one drier than the last. He talked about the marketing budget of Barker Follinge and the percentage that was allocated to fiction; the year-on-year fluctuations in this figure and the projected publicity spend on *The Grass is Greener*. That each number had been plucked from his bitter and jaundiced arse didn't matter. It sounded good and it seemed to work. Lauren was absorbed, listening intently, almost certainly impressed.

As Richard reached the end of his preamble, she shifted in her seat, glanced around the pub and cleared her throat.

'This is all valuable information. But before we go any farther, would you like a drink?'

'Yes,' said Richard, 'yes, I'd love one. A lime and soda, please.'

'Are you sure? Are you not drinking?'

'No, I'm not drinking. I don't, not always. With some people it can be habit forming.'

'Can it really?'

'And anyway, you don't drink. And we're supposed to be in this together.'

'We are, that's true. But I do drink. On special occasions.'

Richard watched as she went to the bar. It was obvious the stats had gone well. Yet although the question of drink had arisen at just the right time – he must have scored some points there too – there was something about Lauren's response that he wasn't entirely comfortable with. Her 'Can it really?' was a pointed comeback, her mention of 'special occasions' designed, he felt, to provoke him into a response. If he didn't know her better, he'd have thought she was up to something.

Lauren came back to their table with a lime and soda and what looked suspiciously like a gin and tonic. He nodded at her glass.

'What's so special about this occasion?'

'I fancy a drink.'

'Is that it?'

'That's it.' Lauren smiled.

'Great,' said Richard, 'well, that's great. Absolutely great. So where were we? Oh yes. Marketing books. There's a few things that I probably should have told you before. For starters, have you wondered why some titles are called bestsellers before they've even been released? Yes? Well, it's because "bestseller" hasn't got anything to do with actual sales. "Bestseller" is just the way publishers classify some of their titles. They're the ones that the publishers push. The ones they have decided they're going to make sell.'

'Really?'

'Really. You see, the thing is, a lot of people think that publishing is about art. About *literature*. But it isn't. Publishing is an industry, just like any other. The industry looks at the public as two groups of people – readers and people who read – and then the industry decides what's going to be read by each group. Now your average 'reader' has the luxury of being better informed about what's going on and so they're reasonably wise to the game. But say you're the sort of person who reads Gary Sayles. Not a reader. Someone who reads. You read what you're told to read. Or at the very least what you're made aware of. The bestsellers. And you're constantly being short-changed because there's a discrepancy between what the industry needs you to read to keep the industry afloat – the units it manufactures, in bulk – and what you might, given half a chance, actually want to read. It's really unhealthy. And it's a vicious circle.'

'I see,' said Lauren. 'But you do realise you're ranting?'

Richard shuffled his paperwork and looked for a graph, a table, anything to give his invective the imprimatur of objective analysis. He settled on a pie chart and waved it in the direction of his newly combative companion.

'Look,' he said, 'this tells you all you need to know.'

'Wait. Let me see. *How Dr Seuss Helped the Berenstain Bears*. Really?'

'Whatever. To get back to my point, it suits the industry to buy into the idea that most people can't cope with better, bigger and, yes, darker books than Sayles'. It's easier that way. It's cheaper and it involves less thought. No one has to judge anything on artistic merit anymore – the only criterion being applied is whether or not they'll make any cash. So people are force-fed the mediocre and sooner or later that's all they want, it's all that's laid out before them and it's all they can take. This deathly drivel.'

'So people don't have a choice about what to read?'

'Not at all. It's just that the presentation of the choice is loaded.'

'Now you're making it sound a bit sinister. Are you saying there's a conspiracy?'

'Not as such. And neither am I saying that people shouldn't try the odd slab of desiccated horseshit once in a while, if that's what they want. It's just that – whatever you're used to – you should be given the option of trying something different every once in a while.'

Hmm. Richard stopped then, puffed out his cheeks, looked around the pub. Suddenly there was a lot to cope with. Lauren, sobriety, gin, it was all getting a bit on top. The cracks were beginning to show, and he could feel far worse than 'desiccated horseshit' bubbling under. Surely he'd done enough by now? Surely it was time Lauren cut him some slack?

'Do you mind if I ask you a question?' she said.

'Oh Christ,' said Richard. 'I recognise that tone of voice.'

'What do you mean?'

'It's your "I've been giving the matter some thought" voice.'

'And?'

'And it's never an idle threat. OK, then. Go ahead.'

'Thank you. I've been thinking about this for a while now. Why do *you* write?'

'Why do *I* write? Blimey. Haven't you got anything easier than that?'

'Oh, I'm sorry. I thought you'd like to talk about it.'

'I suppose, if you must know, I write for the same reason I read. To provoke people. To make them change their way of thinking, to make them laugh. Not chuckle, mind, but wet themselves.'

'I see. And do you think the best way to do this is to bash them over the head?'

'Well, I wouldn't put it like that exactly. But yes, a little bit of shock therapy never hurt anyone.'

Lauren threw her head back and laughed. It was a trilling laugh, a bit forced but inclusive nonetheless. Richard looked at her. What he'd said wasn't that funny.

'That's interesting,' she said. 'But surely life isn't only a choice between putting yourself at risk of SNAPS or being bashed over the head? Aren't the best experiences a mix of all sorts? A mix of the extreme and the ordinary?'

'Maybe.'

'Of the old and the new?'

'Could be.'

'Psychological insight? A little bit of fun?'

'I get the picture,' said Richard. 'But what the hell has this got to do with SNAPS?'

'I'm just thinking about the alternatives to Gary Sayles, that's all. How best to move people on. Because it's not just the great leaps of faith and imagination that move people along, is it? It's how they're assimilated. People change incrementally. And whether or not Gary Sayles is the cause of SNAPS, you may find you have more success altering people's attitudes to that type of writing if you approach the matter in a more reasonable manner rather than bashing them over the head.'

'No,' said Richard, 'you're wrong. People should read books that bash them over the head. If you want to grow, if you want to evolve, then go for it. Be bold. Be daring. Don't hedge your bets.'

'There you go again,' said Lauren. 'You're always so sure of everything. But these are *your* truths, Richard.

Who's to say that the truths you're looking for are the same as those that other people are looking for?'

And at that moment Richard lost it. And it didn't matter whether it was Lauren or Julie or Jeff or his fucking boss or whoever sitting there in front of him, impugning his integrity, wilfully misreading all that he believed in, *taking the piss*. He hadn't stayed off the booze to sit there and be insulted.

'Look. You're not listening to what I'm saying. I mean, yeah, I've no doubt there are some very good reasons why we should all switch off occasionally, kick back with something that isn't going to blow our heads off. A little bit of escapism never hurt anyone. Jesus, I want to escape too. But I want to escape to a place where I might stumble on to a truth or a moment of beauty or darkness, however unwholesome or unpalatable it might be. Where someone tells me something new, or something old in a new way. Not to a land of sludge where anything out of the ordinary is something to be afraid of. Do you understand? I mean really? Do you?'

Richard wiped the corners of his mouth. He looked at Lauren and swallowed hard. He was suddenly drained.

'Look,' he said. 'It's getting late. I ought to be going.'

'I'm just about finished,' said Lauren, raising her eyebrows, 'we could share a taxi...'

She reached out to touch his arm, stopped herself, pulled her hand away. Jesus, Richard thought, she's only bleedin' drunk.

'No,' he said, 'I need to go straight home. Tomorrow I'll speak to the press. I've got an in with the *Correspondent* so I'll start there. Then I'll call you.'

And with that, he stood up, drained his lime and soda and left the pub.

Lauren waited outside the station in the queue for a cab, among the drunks and the shouts and the laughter. It had been a good night. She was pleased with herself. Short of actually raising her middle finger to Richard, she couldn't have done more to let him know that she was not going to put up with any more of his mindless provocations.

She'd promised herself that she was going to have fun and she had. She'd knocked back the gin – she must have had at least three – and copied his direct approach to the conversation. She'd even ventured a few jokes. She supposed her own behaviour could almost have been called provocative. It had certainly been the first time in, well, *yonks* that she felt as though she had any power over a man. And *that* was fun.

Lauren was tipsy. She would need to consider it all later. A taxi came and she sat back in her seat. She looked out of the window at the city. 'Where to?' asked the driver. She pretended for a moment not to have heard. They drove slowly around the one-way system, stopping and starting. So this was what it felt like to be free.

It wasn't until she was almost home that the tears came, in slow salty drops that she made no effort to wipe away.

In which Richard speaks to the national press

Alistair Bevan was proud to call himself a literary man. The appellation was nothing more than the due recognition of his standing within the culture. In the years since he had read Russian at Oxford, his steadily jowling mugshot, authoritative byline and confident tone had graced the books pages of some of the most prestigious publications in the country. Now, as Literary Editor of the *Correspondent*, Alistair Bevan was a bone fide member of the literary establishment.

For some, the very idea of a literary establishment was anathema. Its role was much – and in many cases wilfully – misunderstood. Alistair knew the naysayers' objections were many. Principal among those directed at him daily – by email and letters that may have been scrawled in green ink – was a criticism of the system that resulted in the books pages of the *Correspondent* being the exclusive preserve of a 'Dynastic Mafia'. Judging by the unexceptional nature of their prose, the complainants argued, most *Correspondent* reviewers seemed to have got their commissions by virtue of their name alone. Were they not the sons and daughters of columnists, authors and editors? Members of an elite? Was it not about time that Alistair gave a fair crack of the whip to others? Those who weren't 'connected' but had instead been to redbrick universities or spent years honing their craft on blogs or, say, the *Chorlton Gazette* or *Nether Wallop Bugle*?

Alistair found such criticisms naive. They were missing the point. He looked at it this way (and really, the reasoning was infallible): just as democracy needed checks and balances to keep the barbarians away from the gates, so the culture required gatekeepers to look after the upkeep of the artistic landscape of the nation. Mediators, critics and arbiters – call them what you will – these people *were* an elite by any other name. But what of it? People didn't buy newspapers just to be informed but to be persuaded into a way of thinking. And who was better placed to persuade, the scions of the literary nobility or the enthusiastic semi-professionals of the population at large?

There was also, apparently, an issue with the regions. Alistair was often contacted by people who ran small provincial publishing houses. They were largely humourless people, plugging this dialect-driven curiosity of a novel or that socially realistic memoir, while muttering darkly about the dangers of 'regionalism', whatever that might be. They would criticise the *Correspondent* too, this time for its attitude to independent publishing. This was to criticise a dog for not being a cat. The *Correspondent* did not offer a benevolent service, it was not a charitable venture. It wasn't as if he didn't care. Alistair had supped – literally – with some of London's finest small-press people. But there was a limit. Publishing was an industry that was operating at capacity. The number of titles published already outstripped the hours of reading time available in the population at large. What was the point of reviewing titles that were going to be read by only a handful of people?

One of Alistair's more consistently annoying epistlers was a blogger – and wannabe member of the literary elite – by the name of Richard Anger. Over many years the fellow had seen fit to litter Alistair's inbox with links to under-informed rants on what constituted 'good' literature. He'd also submitted an equal number of unsolicited reviews.

His latest words landed with a greater than usual thump on Alistair's virtual doorstep. It was a long and involved email concerning the 'public health implications' of a forthcoming novel. In it, he'd asked Alistair to run a news story in the next issue. 'Anything you can do to help bring this to the attention of the public,' he'd said, 'would be welcome at this stage. We are talking about averting a potential catastrophe.'

Alistair knew enough about the hyperbolic argot of the bloggerati to question the accuracy of this assertion. And besides. While the basic premise of Anger's argument was preposterous enough – an unsubstantiated claim about the damaging effects of certain books – the pest was once again misreading the needs of the *Correspondent* and the role of Alistair therein. If the accusations *were* provable – and mediocre art could in some way harm people – then surely the danger would not be restricted to books? Exposure to mediocre TV programmes, advertising campaigns, films and music would prove to be equally hazardous. And then how on earth would the *Correspondent* fill its weekend lifestyle supplements?

More pertinently, this Mr Anger seemed to be

implying that Alistair should have an opinion on the reading habits of the general populace. As a Literary Man, Alistair held no such views. There were people lost in the cultural landscape, who were beyond help, people whom not even the *Correspondent* could reach. There was no debate about what these people could and should read. They were beyond consideration. This constituency would – and did – read anything. As long as they kept buying books it was of no consequence what books they bought and no one who understood the industry – no one who was worthy of Alistair's time – would dream of suggesting otherwise...

Photographs without people in them

Lauren listened to the message and smiled.

'Hello, Prof, it's Richard. I think we need to think again. I wrote to various people in the nationals and they're just not biting. If we're going to get people's attention we need a rethink. I've got one or two suggestions that I think we migh... shit... I'm running out of cred—'

So. A rethink. If Richard's previous mood swings were anything to go by, they'd be back on terrible truths again by now. Was she in the mood for terrible truths? It was hard to know. As the new, single-digit-waving Lauren she was certainly open to the idea that she might be. She switched off her phone, poured herself a glass of red wine and sat back on her sofa. Warmed by the wine and the late afternoon sun that came full and strong into her front room, Lauren closed her eyes and thought about the motivations and behaviour of this uniquely confusing man.

Some people, she knew, needed no one else. They were satisfied with their own company and their own counsel. Since Will's death, she'd counted herself as one of them. Others craved the approval of friends or colleagues and bent their character to the prevailing mores, in order to fit in. Richard, on the other hand, seemed to be different again. He was uncompromisingly himself but also seemed in permanent need of validation. As if he was afraid that he would amount to nothing if people did not accept him for his essential difference.

At least that was how he had at first appeared. Lately there had been a shift in his attitude. Lauren had noticed it last night: he was really making an effort. His sobriety hadn't been entirely convincing and he'd tried to underpin his observations with a pseudo-empirical analysis that had been bewildering and at times frankly bizarre. But he was trying hard and she appreciated it. Despite previous evidence to the contrary – his disastrous attempt to impress her with his fiction, for example – he had obviously been paying attention to what she said and to the way she thought. To her...

The world Lauren lived in had long been one of fixed points of reference and lines of light. Photography and buildings and the natural world, these had been her passions. If you could call them that. She had taken the occasional leap of faith, at least in her work – she was a scientist, she had to – but even with the uncertainty that this brought, hers had been a world that could – and needed to – be ordered.

Since she had first read about SNAPS, however, Lauren had been immersed in an entirely new environment. The world of books was a heady miasma of emotional high-wire acts and intellectual challenges and moral conundrums. She'd been exposed to contradictions, fertile and enticing. Seen the possibilities of the unexpected, the potential in the – now what was that word again? – the transgressive.

She had begun to think differently, behave differently, even use language differently. To revisit a long-buried lyrical sensibility. To have fun. She had given the finger to the world, sworn, revelled in the role of conversational provocateur. Slowly, incrementally, new connections were being made in her neural circuitry. Her experiment was beginning to produce results. A transformation was under way. And at the centre of this transformation, for all of his inchoate messy whims and drunken telephone messages, was Richard.

Lauren opened her eyes. She took another sip from her glass and picked up her camera. Lauren hadn't taken many photographs recently. It had been the longest hiatus that she could remember. Ordinarily she'd have given herself a hard time about her lack of creative activity but this time she had been creative in other areas. Now, though, it was time to return to her art.

It was dusk. She walked to the park. The pavement was wet and there was moisture in the air. Lauren smelled damp leaves and rotting wood. The clouds were low but the sun glowed brilliantly through a gap in the grey and the autumnal evening gloom was iridescent, blushed with cherry and violet and streaked with orange. The light was eerie, otherworldly.

There were many trees in the park. There were birch and lime and fir and spruce. Lauren often took photographs here on Sunday mornings in winter when lovers were out walking among the skeletal forms. This evening, the leaves were still thick and the light played around the edges of the trees and dark bushes and swept luminously across the grass, out of the shadows of the clouds. She saw a horse chestnut, verdant and brilliantly yellow veined. Lauren looked for subject matter among the greenery but it was the light that she wanted to record. There were no people, but she didn't need to capture people, not today.

She walked along mulch-covered paths. She shot half a roll of film and then a misty rain began to fall. She turned her face to the sky until it was wet and she was refreshed and then she switched off her camera and headed home.

In which Richard sends
Lauren a poem

Another day, another email.

Hello Lauren
Just a quick one. I'm sorry about the other
night; I realise I got a bit aerated there. I'm sorry
about drawing a blank with the press too. We
really do have to move quickly now, somehow
and soon.

In the meantime, here's a poem I thought you
might like. It's not your usual (not that I'm sure
what your usual is) but it is one of my favourites,
from back in the day. And in case you think I'm
going soft in my old age, I'm not. The man was
a surrealist. Beyond that, I'm not going to say
anything else. Please take it any way you like.
Except the wrong one, of course...

Richard Anger Esq,
The Attic,
Harborne etc.

I have Dreamed of you so Much – Robert Desnos

I have dreamed of you so much that you are no
    longer real.
Is there still time for me to reach your breathing
    body, to kiss your mouth and make
your dear voice come alive again?

I have dreamed of you so much that my arms,
    grown used to being crossed on my
chest as I hugged your shadow, would perhaps not
    bend to the shape of your body.
For faced with the real form of what has haunted
    me and governed me for so many
days and years, I would surely become a shadow.

O scales of feeling.

I have dreamed of you so much that surely there is
    no more time for me to wake up.
I sleep on my feet prey to all the forms of life and
    love, and you, the only one who
counts for me today, I can no more touch your face
    and lips than touch the lips and
face of some passerby.

I have dreamed of you so much, have walked so
    much, talked so much, slept so much
with your phantom, that perhaps the only thing left
    for me is to become a phantom
among phantoms, a shadow a hundred times more
    shadow than the shadow that moves and goes
    on moving, brightly, over the sundial of your life.

Lauren read the poem three times.

The first time, it didn't make much sense. The second time, a meaning appeared, of sorts, then shimmied enticingly out of reach. The third time she understood and her stomach lurched, almost as it might when you are driving along and you crest the brow of a dip in the road. Except this time there was no end to the sensation; instead the feeling welled until it engulfed her. It came from no sense or reason, it felt like something close to helplessness and it brought her, overwhelmed and teetering, to the edge of her experiment's most terrifying intimation yet...

Gary tells Mike and Susan how it is

That evening Zeke and Pippa arrive at Gary Sayles' house. It is a Georgian end-of-terrace with steps leading up to a wide front door. There are black railings.

Zeke is Mike, Pippa is losing sight of Susan. They are winging it in pantomime Method style. Pippa is wearing a gingham frock and trainers. Dorothy from *The Wizard of Oz* meets Lily Allen. Zeke is wearing what he wore when they last met Gary Sayles. Zeke thinks that Pippa is taking the piss but he can't decide whether he thinks this because of the gingham or the trainers.

Pippa climbs the steps, pushes an enormous brass doorbell. They wait. Gary Sayles opens the door. He is wearing a thick red Pierre Cardin dressing gown with gold tassels and a green plastic visor. He is part asexual Hugh Heffner, part clean-shaven Howard Hughes. He is clearly a man in the middle of a carefully planned mission.

'Hello... I'm sorry, I've forgotten your names?'

'Mike.'

'Susan.'

'Mike, Susan,' Gary says, as he ushers them inside, 'come this way.'

'Thank you,' says Mike.

'Most kindly,' murmurs Pippa.

Zeke shoots a glance at Pippa but it is OK that she is not quite with it; Gary Sayles is not listening. The three of them pass through a wide hallway. The walls are colourless. There are cornices and coving. There are tall plants in pots. A child's tricycle protrudes from a doorway but there is no personality to the space. It is decorated like the lobby of a small hotel.

Gary's voice seems to have dropped an octave since the last time they met. He is speaking more slowly than before.

'We'll talk in my study,' he says.

The three of them move up a staircase. They pass a proudly framed Monet.

'Ah, Monet,' says Gary, 'such a wonderful use of...'

'Light?' says Mike.

'Paint?' suggests Pippa.

'Subject matter,' says Gary Sayles. 'He painted pictures of flowers and ponds, nothing more complicated than that. And people still buy them. Do you know why? Because flowers and ponds are part of a universal language. From the highest mountain to the driest desert, everyone likes flowers and ponds.'

Gary pauses to let this sink in. Pippa understands its significance in an instant. The boy is a piece of work beyond her most wishful dreams. Pure class. She checks the weight of her shoulder bag. The camera is still there. Still rolling.

On the landing, they wait outside a door.

'Brace yourselves,' says Gary. 'For this is the factory of dreams.'

Gary's study is small. There is a large window overlooking the street. A Mac sits on a desk. The desk is of functional design. It is covered with photos in plain clip-in frames. They are neatly arranged. They look newly wiped. The whole room looks newly wiped. There is the smell of chemical-fresh air. There is a photograph of Gary posing with a football on a football pitch in a football stadium. He looks awkward. There is a photo of a small child who looks a bit like Gary. He looks as though he is looking for something that isn't there. There is a photo of Gary with his arm around the DJ Danny Kelly.

Mike's attention is taken by a soft toy sitting on the corner of the desk.

'Ah,' says Gary to Mike. 'Barney the Bear. Do you remember?'

'The dream sequence?' says Mike. 'From *Cutting the Cake*?'

'I have chosen well,' says Gary.

Against one of the walls there is a stand-alone bookcase. It is filled with copies of Gary's novels, books by Paulo Coehlo and Susan Jeffers. Hanging above the desk is a sequential arrangement of his covers. *Our Legendary Twenties* has been called 'wry, bittersweet and unashamedly sentimental' while *Cutting the Cake* has been likened to 'a holiday read for the comfort of your own home'. By the time of *Man, Woman, Baby, The Bookshop Magazine* has christened him the 'Populist Laureate'. Mike looks on approvingly. Pippa feels her blood rising. Her heart beats faster.

'Before we start, there's something you should know,' says Gary. He crosses to the window with his hands behind his back. As though he has practised the move.

'The time has come for me to move out of the city. There are too many distractions here. This won't affect you, of course, for I will continue to write about the concerns of the people. But if I am to preserve my creative dignity – if I am to keep sight of the broader view – there has to be some distance between us. Accessibility is all very well but when you are as successful as I am, there comes a time when you have to accept that your life is not the life of an ordinary person. To pretend otherwise would be dishonest. It's Catch-22. The more I appeal to ordinary people, the farther away from them I get.'

'How do you cope with that?' asks Mike.

'We all have our crosses to bear,' says Gary. 'Anyway. On to business. Please take a seat. The launch of the People's Literature Tour will go ahead as planned, a week on Saturday. The other day I found an ideal venue. A church near St Pancras. I'm working on the later dates as we speak. I'm thinking of concentrating on London for the time being. There'll be one in the west, one in the east and one in the north. That way we don't leave anyone out. We can see to the regions when they demand a piece of the action; you'll have to keep an eye on the website for that.

'As we've discussed, Mike, you'll do the first reading, Susan the next and so on. As far as my presence goes, I'll be there on the first night but after that it's all down to you. You'll be my representatives. With that in mind, I'd like you to wear these.'

Gary reaches into a desk drawer and fetches out two T-shirts.

'They're going to be on sale on the night. They

are the first in a series of promotional lines I've got in the pipeline. Nothing too over the top. At all times you must remember this isn't about celebrity, it's not about Gary Sayles the man, the personality. It's about more than that. It's about Gary Sayles the writer.'

Mike nods his head at this. Pippa thinks it is now time to strike up the bong.

'Mr Sayles, er, Gary?' says Susan. 'We were wondering if you'd mind us filming each other on the tour. We'd like some sort of a record. To remind us of working with you.'

'Yes, yes, some grainy handheld footage. I like it. In fact you may want to get some of me in there as well. Put it into context. Put me down for a copy of the finished product, will you? There may be merchandising opportunities.'

'You can count on it,' says Pippa, under her voice, and then Susan pipes up, 'Oh yes sir, you can count on that all right.'

'Pippa...' says Zeke.

'Pippa?' says Susan.

'Susan,' says Mike, 'look, if it's OK with Gary I think we should be going. I am rather tired, after all.'

'Ah, but aren't you forgetting something?' says Gary. 'I have something you might need.'

From the desk he takes a book and gives it to Mike. It is a finished copy of *The Grass is Greener*.

'Treat it well,' says Gary, and he smiles the smile of an unfunny man. 'I know I'm asking a lot of you to finish it in a week and be ready to give a reading. But something tells me you're the man for the job.'

Mike says, 'I'll try my best...' and Pippa drops her bag.

'And now?' says Gary. 'Now you may go.'

Mike is shown to the door. Pippa crosses to the other side of the room and feigns interest in the montage of book covers on the wall. With Gary waiting by the door, she drops her letter on his desk. Bows her head, shuffles past him. As the three of them come down the stairs and into the hallway, a woman carrying a large child emerges from the room with the trike in it.

'Gary?' says the woman.

Mike thinks that she looks like a woman who has not been getting the right sort of attention from her husband. Pippa thinks she looks like trouble. Gary doesn't catch her eye.

Pippa and Zeke are confused

On the way home Pippa has a funny turn. She is massively stoned. The street lights and traffic lights and the lights from cars blaze in the city's murk. They spark into each other, catching fire like panics screaming for attention at the edge of her consciousness and then burning out. It had been so simple. Show up the fool and his art for what it is. But Gary Sayles worries Pippa. He is too much. He must know who they are and what they do. He must be using them. Playing them for putzes. Or yutzes. Or klutzes. Maybe he'll turn up to the first reading of the People's Literature Tour with his own camera crew. Film them filming him. Are she and Zeke to be the victims of a post-pre-ironic irony that is so delicious, fragrant and melodic that they will never be able to put pen to paper, no, *thought* to a *variety of media* again? Is it a bluff? A double bluff, a counter-bluff? Is Gary Sayles' art perfection?

The moment is truly fearful. It possesses the horror of a never-ending sequence, of infinity squared.

Then there is her new plan. Susan as besotted fan, Pippa as artist, fucking the novelist and his very idea of Art. On paper this is Kool and the Gang. But in reality? What was she thinking? Why did she not talk it over with Zeke?

Pippa's brain is jelly. It is being poked. It is being flat-smacked by wooden bats. Acid-laced red-haired children are having their way with her brain. Her brain hurts. Pippa takes Zeke's hand. She needs him here just now...

The moment passes. The cars and the streets come back into focus. Gary Sayles is a man-boy, a sap once more. Pippa will be nominated for awards.

Zeke has been oblivious to Pippa's scare. He is thinking about reading some of *The Grass is Greener* when he gets home. He is not planning on staying up too long. He is going to surprise Pippa the next morning. It has been a long time since they have had sex in the missionary position, him on top, no props, no moves, no toys. Just plugging away. He thinks it will make a nice change.

Fictional lives

Amy Sayles woke at seven the following day to find
Gary already dressing. Within ten minutes he had left
the house. She didn't ask him where he was going.
He'd have only said something 'enigmatic' and she'd
had her fill of that. She had more important things on
her mind. Because this time she knew her husband
wasn't coming back.

Recently there had been rows, the first bad feeling of their marriage. 'We never know where you are
from one day to the next,' she'd told him a week ago,
'Garfield hasn't seen you since last Thursday. It's not
good enough.' Gary had responded by crossing to the
window of their bedroom and intoning sonorously,
'But Amy. The children of artists have to bear their
crosses too.'

Another time she'd said, 'We don't stay up late
talking any more,' not because she had particularly
enjoyed staying up late talking, but because it had
been an indication that in his interpretation of their
life, all was well between them. 'That's because I'm
moving on, to bigger horizons. We have nothing to
talk about,' he'd said, and she'd said, 'I know that.
That's not the point.'

Amy had decided to retake control of the situation.
Later that day, while Gary was grabbing a shower
'between meetings', she asked him whether there
was someone else. She had sounded matter-of-fact

about it and in a way she was. At least then she would know what she was dealing with. Gary came out of the shower slowly, almost regally. And told Amy that she was beginning to sound like Lucy.

Lucy is a character in *The Grass is Greener*. She is the wife of Ben, the narrator. She is described as plain. She likes to play board games. When Ben has an affair, Lucy is at first distraught. Then she decides she can't live without him and wants him back.

Amy was furious. Gary avoiding her question was one thing. But if his idea of their marriage was now so far removed from reality that he was regarding Amy as a Lucy – a cipher with no interior life who was defined by her relationship to men – well, that was unforgivable.

Amy knew how relationships between men and women always ended. Their stories became incompatible. She had thought that Gary's lack of imagination meant that they could be an exception to the rule. That whatever narratives she created to get herself by, his would keep him happily chugging alongside. But it wasn't to be. He had been living for so long in his two-dimensional world that it had turned him into an arsehole.

And wherever he was, he wasn't coming back.

In which books help Richard to overcome an existential crisis

Three days later review copies of *The Grass is Greener* began to arrive at newspaper offices, bookshops and the homes of bloggers. Within twelve hours the reviewers began to die.

A pointlessly detailed passage in Chapter 3, in which the hero of the piece argues with his wife during a Bank Holiday trip to IKEA, accounted for a part-time critic-about-town on the *Bristol Evening Star*; Chapter 4's barely credible description of a drunken seduction and one-night-stand did for a contributor to *Beach Reads R Us!*; and the Books Editor of the *Glasgow Chronicle* passed away after becoming cognitively becalmed during the course of a particularly laborious pun in Chapter 5.

The deaths were not confined to reviewers. A cleaner in cahoots with the postboy on the *Manchester Telegraph* succumbed to a conversation about TV theme tunes between two men supposedly sitting in a pub, and the death of the sixteen-year-old son of the owner of the popular site *What's Booking?* was directly attributable to his exposure to the fourth in a series of observations about the time it takes women to leave the house...

A copy of the novel arrived at Back Street Books with the morning's post and it was just what Richard needed. Because that morning, he was in the clammy grip of an existential crisis.

Its catalyst was Lauren. His relationship with the woman had gone completely wankytits, and not in a good way either. Every one of his romantic gambits had been dismissed with a sort of high-class meh. Most of these rejections Richard could ascribe to poor execution of potty wheezes. But Lauren had played her part too, by virtue of playing no discernible part at all. In the time he had known her, she had run the gamut of emotions from coolly aloof through disarmingly distant to bewilderingly together. Occasionally he'd detect a scintilla of annoyance but that was as far as it went; there had been no signs of substantial disquiet, nothing for Richard to push at, no buttons on her façade. Instead he had been throwing himself against a wall on which the only impression he had left was a series of cartoon face prints. And now he was exhausted and mind-fucked and existentially done...

Then he opened the package, saw the book. Its cover, shining with spangly malevolence, was embossed with an illustration of a leather jacket, torn in two. It was accompanied by an invitation to 'The People's Literature Tour', a press release and a photograph entitled, *Hello!*-style, 'The Author at Home with Wife Amy and Son Garfield'. For a moment Richard allowed himself to be diverted by this soft-focus horror. It was a picture of domestic bliss, its duplicitous nature betrayed only by the look on the face of Sayles' wife. Richard recognised the expression and – surprisingly – the woman too. He wondered where he had seen her before; doubtless it would have been at a pub or party, back in the day. Then he picked up the press release.

'A man who has it all... the passing of time... recapture his youth,' he read, 'Ben and Lucy split up... blah blah... divide belongings... fuckity blah... favourite Coldplay album, *Love Story* DVD, pot plant...'

Jesus please no...

Richard didn't need to read the book – shitballs, he wasn't about to read the book – to see that here was the antithesis of everything a novel should be. The cover alone told him that. In the course of his work, he'd seen the like too many times before. This was a book written by rules. A desecration of the printed word. Mediocrity at its most virulently offensive. At its most obscene.

Richard knew that books could be mediocre. And he knew that mediocrity in books was not just confined to insipid male confessionals. There was mediocrity in misery memoirs and sagas about dragons and goblins and expats having humorous experiences and dour or feisty detectives and magic-realist Anglo-Indian high-caste post-colonial allegories and novels full of nothing but vacuous po-mo trickery. And as for the undead. Don't even get him started on the fucking undead. Yet none of this stuff had stained the pages of books with a more insidious stain than the works of the murderous bastard Sayles. None of this stuff had presented the fight against mediocrity and all it stood for as such an obvious case of life or death.

Richard threw the book across the shop and snarled into his next piece of post. It was the local listings mag. Here was more of the same, mediocre musicals adapted from mediocre albums, mediocre films from mediocre books. Then something caught his eye. 'Artists for Hire...' it said. 'Flash Mobs and Spectacles for the Non-Discerning Punter.' And Richard had a revelation. What he could do – no, what he had to do – about every last little damnable thing in the world.

Books. That was what this was about. That was what it all came back to. SNAPS, his non-fuck two-step with Lauren, even, at a stretch, him and Julie; all of it started with books and how they'd made him feel and behave and what they'd brought to his life and the lives of other people. The rest was incidental. And as Richard stood there in the dim lighting of the last little bookshop in town, he saw blazing before him the prospect of the ultimate provocation, of vengeance, sweet vengeance against the world, and of the return of his purpose in a fiery and glorious rush of will...

Richard made a phone call to the Barker Follinge distributor. He asked for fifty copies of *The Grass is Greener*. That should be plenty. They checked his credit rating, said they'd get back to him. The deal was okayed. He arranged for the delivery to be made to the first venue of 'The People's Literature Tour'. Then he picked up the listings magazine and dialled the number on the advert in the smalls.

'Hello,' he said, to an enthusiastic Pippa, 'I wonder if you can help me. I've just seen your advert and I think you're just the thing I'm looking for...'

Fifteen minutes later he finished his conversation and dialled Lauren.

Burning books

'Lauren? It's Richard. I've got a plan. We're going to burn the books.'

'What?'

'We're going to go to London and burn the books.'

'But why?'

'Because I've decided, that's why. Well, you helped me decide as it goes. It came to me this morning. In a bookcase at your house, with all that other old-skool historical gubbins. The Savonarola.'

'I'm not with you...'

'You had a copy of the *Life of Savonarola*. On your shelf. In your back room. Haven't you read it?'

'No. It's not mine. I mean, it belonged to someone else.'

'Whatever. It gave me an idea. *The* idea. Savonarola was a priest who was connected to the Borgias. His thing was burning books. Well, books and other things actually. Anything he considered sinful in fact. And we're going to do the same. It'll be great, trust me.'

'I see. But isn't it a little extreme?'

'I don't care. The book is going to be launched in about a week's time and we need to be down there making a noise, warning people off the thing. So. Are you with me?'

Lauren nearly makes a move

'Richard? It's Lauren.'

'I know. Didn't we just...? You know... Get off the phone to each other?'

'Yes. But there's something I forgot to mention. I've been thinking—'

'Oh, Christ—'

'No. Not like that. It's just this whole SNAPS business. The number of people who could be at risk. It's enormous. And it's been difficult. For both of us. We've both been working on it for weeks now – in our spare time – and I think we need to be careful not to lose ourselves to it. We owe ourselves a break, don't you think? So, anyway. I... I mean we... I mean there's an exhibition on at the Ikon Gallery. And I was wondering if you'd like to go?'

'Blimey. Are you asking me out?'

'Certainly not.'

'Because it sounds like you're asking me out.'

'Richard?'

'Only if you're asking me out—'

'I'm going to hang up in a min—'

'OK, OK. Yes, I'd love to.'

A date?

As Lauren walked out of town to the Ikon Gallery, she found herself dwelling on the implications of her invitation to Richard. She had meant what she'd said on the phone; the two of them *were* in need of some relief from their work on SNAPS. But there was also some truth in Richard's suggestion too. It certainly *felt* as though she was asking him out. Was it possible she'd invited him as a direct consequence of the poem he'd sent her? Her reaction to it had certainly shocked her. Then again, despite being initially overwhelmed, she'd regained a sense of perspective. Even as she'd teetered, she'd taken a step back and then another, until she had regained her emotional decorum.

Whatever the thinking behind her proposition, the gallery wasn't providing the distraction she'd hoped for. Arriving early, she made her way to the bar, ordered a coffee and sat down at a table. The bar was busy. Two people were sitting at the counter on stools. Tapas was being served and even though it was in between what Lauren would have thought of as lunch and dinnertime, the place was doing brisk business. She watched as trays went out from the kitchen behind the bar, small terracotta dishes of olives or prawns decorated with chopped red chilli or dusted with what she presumed was paprika, plates of steaming fried whitebait to share. And she was captured and taken back to Corfu and to a taverna, a death and a book.

It got worse. Lauren sighed, rubbed the back of her neck with her hand and opened a catalogue. All she knew of the exhibition was that it was a retrospective by a local Turner-nominated photographer. Reading the notes, she realised that even this choice was fraught with unforeseen intrusions.

The catalogue showed a series of dour landscapes featuring brownbelt sites, recaptured and feral wasteland and the odd corrugated-iron storage shed. It was singular work. There were none of the occasional splashes of colour – on vehicles or buildings or skips – that lesser artists might have used to bring into relief the drab, washed-out greens and browns of the muddied grass and low industrial skies; there were no sudden man-made edges or angles, no contrasts to bring you up against a violent visual anomaly. This was art as a recording of the ordinary.

And that was the problem. The representation of the 'ordinary' was an issue that lay at the heart of any theoretical understanding of SNAPS. And given Richard's professed antipathy to such a literal approach to art – and her defence of it – he would surely regard the choice of exhibition as a provocative act. Talk about bashing a man over the head...

She sipped her coffee, checked her watch against the clock behind the bar. Richard was late. She told herself it didn't matter. Richard was always late. Rubbed her palms together, pressed her fingers to her lips as if in prayer. Then he arrived.

He sat down at Lauren's table. He looked twitchy. She wondered whether he had been drinking again. It didn't seem so. His skin didn't look healthy and his face was drawn but his eyes were bright. She thought they might be brighter than she'd ever seen them, then she realised she'd never really looked at them before, not that closely.

'Hello, Richard,' said Lauren. 'Before we start, can I make a proposal? I've made some discoveries this week and I'd like to share them with you. But I meant what I said about needing a break. So can I suggest we steer clear of SNAPS, just for the next hour or so?'

'By all means,' said Richard. 'Let's talk about something other than books. Something safer. Like politics or religion.'

They set off at regulation art gallery pace into the main room of the exhibition. Lauren felt uncomfortable moving so slowly. Their stately progress seemed to thicken further the air between them and exaggerate Richard's cocking of his head, his frowns and tuts. If he was as nervous as she was, his demeanour was more convincingly relaxed.

'What do you think?' asked Lauren. 'About the photographs?'

'What do I think?' said Richard, and she was surprised at how relieved she was to see him smile. 'I think it shows how we have to be careful not to expect too much or judge too quickly. Because if we do, important stuff gets overlooked. I think it's about how lots of things are interesting, that we don't have to go to the edge to find truths about life. I also think that you could have been a bit more subtle.'

'What do you mean?' said Lauren, pleased that he had picked up on her error of judgement.

'We said no books chat, didn't we?' said Richard.

'Well, that includes books chat dressed up as 'what-do-you-think-of-the-photography?' chat.'

'Oh. Yes. I see what you mean,' said Lauren. 'When you put it like that, though, it's difficult, isn't it? Avoiding books chat, I mean.'

'It certainly presupposes we have other things to talk about.'

Now it was her turn to smile. She touched him tentatively on the shoulder and left her hand there. Richard turned his whole body to her. He was very close. He looked her in the eye, with a seriousness that seemed like intent. Moved closer still.

'Without scaring each other off, I mean,' he said.

Lauren took a step back. 'Not at all!' she said, maybe too enthusiastically. 'A little bit of fear is good for you.'

'Well, it gets you going, doesn't it? Provokes a response. And you like provocative, don't you?'

His tone was mocking but warm. She withdrew a little further and gathered herself, even as she sensed she mustn't let him have the better of this exchange.

'I won't say it doesn't have its attractions... in the right sort of people, of course, in small doses,' she said, and was pleased with the pauses and the assertiveness she brought to them. 'But you can have too much of anything, can't you?'

'Blimey. There's just no avoiding this book chat, is there?'

This time they both smiled. They looked at the last of the exhibition, then continued into the bar. As Richard fetched two glasses of wine, Lauren sat at the table and thought about where her experiment would take her next.

'Cheers,' said Richard. 'Is that it, then? Are we done?'

'What do you mean?'

'With the photographs?'

'I suppose so.'

'Good. Then can I make a proposal too?'

'Please do.'

'OK. I think the time has come. Whatever happens with SNAPS, I think we should just get on with it.'

'Get on with what?'

'This. All this. Whatever this is.'

'Whatever what is?'

'This! You and me.'

'I honestly wouldn't know where to start,' said Lauren.

'I know what you mean,' he said. 'It's been quite an experience one way or another, hasn't it? Or series of ongoing experiences.'

'It has. A mix of the extreme, if you like, and the ordinary—'

'The old and the new—'

'The old and the new.'

'And what was it? Ah, yes. Psychological insight and a little bit of fun. Just a little bit of fun, mind you,' said Richard. 'We can't be too reckless, now, can we? I suppose my point is that it's been a bit of an eye-opener for me and I don't want it to stop when we haven't gotten anywhere yet. I reckon it's time to change gear. To see what this all turns into.'

Lauren blushed. That's enough for now, she thought, and decided to rein herself in. She was happy with the way things had gone but if they had to 'get on with it', they could do so at her pace. With a 'hmm' that she tried to make distracted rather than non-committal, she returned to her programme. Richard, wrong-footed by this sudden reintroduction to her froideur, consoled himself by toying with the menu. Every so often he made an interested noise, like a child seeking attention. Then he appeared to shrug, and stopped.

They finished their wine in silence and headed for the exit. On the way out, they stopped at the shop in the foyer of the gallery. It was small and well stocked with coffee-table books and monographs and catalogues. As Richard browsed the photography and Lauren looked at a guide to Japanese screen prints, a thought occurred to her, one that might help her with future gallery trips or more.

'Richard? You just said that investigating SNAPS has been a bit of an eye-opener. Would you say it's changed you?'

'I hope so. It's nice to think you change with each new experience. But you never know, do you? What about you?'

'Certainly. Certainly. I don't know exactly how, but...'

At this, Richard had his attention taken by something over Lauren's shoulder.

'Hold that thought,' he said, and slid past her, crossing quickly to a man on the other side of the shop. The man had his back to them. He was dressed in old denim and was holding an enormous carrier bag from a DIY chain. Lauren watched as Richard spoke to him. They were talking quietly and she couldn't hear what was being said. The man shrugged and Richard shook his head. The man looked over his shoulder and around the shop and rummaged in his bag. Then he put something back on the shelf – Lauren couldn't see what – said something else to Richard and hurried out of the shop.

Richard rejoined Lauren.

'I'm sorry about that,' he said.

'What were you doing?'

'Oh, nothing. That fella was just about to steal a book. A big, expensive book. I was going to turn a blind eye, but it's a bit more complicated than that, isn't it? Because this is an independent art gallery and it can't afford losses like that.'

'I see,' said Lauren. 'That's very observant of you. And it's good you did the right thing.'

'I thought that,' said Richard. 'But anyway. Where were we? Have I changed? And how? It's difficult to say, isn't it? Only time will tell, I guess.'

He reached over and kissed her then, quickly and on the side of her mouth. It felt natural and Lauren wondered whether she should kiss him back and then it was too late and she hadn't.

Interview with a writer

'Hello? Yes, this is Gary Sayles. Hermione Bevan-Jones? OK. Yes, I've asked for the interview to be brought forward because I had what you might call a bit of a revelation the other day and I thought I'd strike while the iron was hot. Well, in a way it's to do with the People's Literature Tour. You got the press release about that, then? Good. I insisted on writing some of that myself this time around. Just to make sure my side of the story got heard. "You won't know whether to laugh or cry"? That was mine. But there's more to what I've got to say than that, much more. First things first. How is *The Magazine* set up for this thing? Do I have the cover? Good, good. I'll sort you out with a few portraits and some for this interview as well. No, no, not at all. I insist. As I said, I'm taking a more active interest in my publicity. It's all about authors being more hands-on now, or hadn't you heard? Yes, that's right. It's because of the internet. Anyway, I've got more than enough shots to cover any angle. Just let me know what you'll need. I've got funny, approachable, serious. Or all three. Maybe approachable on the cover, funny in the index and serious in the inter – OK. Do you think so? Are you sure? OK, I'll leave you to it. By the way, I spoke to Alistair there the other day. On the books desk. He was saying he was having a bit of difficulty finding a reviewer for the novel. Something to do with his writers saying that they didn't think that they could do it justice in print. Do you know if he's managed to sort it yet? Because it should really run in the same edition as the interview. Right. Oh, I see. He found someone but he's got a bit of work to do on the review? Yes. Yes. Tone it down a bit. I daresay. I understand. I suppose for a lot of freelancers getting that quote on the cover is as close as they're going to get to the real thing, isn't it? I mean, you have to get noticed somehow and I suppose a bit of harmless exaggeration usually does the trick. But you do work quite closely with Alistair, you can keep me posted? Good. OK. I'm sorry? He's your what? Your father? Oh, I see. I might have guessed. No, no, nothing like that. I mean, yes, I used to have a problem with that. A bit of a chip on my shoulder, you might say. In the past – yes, I admit it – I've had a go at the literary excesses of the so-called elite. I hated their fancy cliques and fancy new words, y'know, I really resented their snobbery. Do you know the trouble my agent had in getting the so-called "serious" press interested in what I was doing? Even after the public's response to *Cutting the Cake*? But I understand things a little bit better now, about writing and what it means to be a writer. Which is one of the things I wanted to talk to you about today. So, before we start, do you have any questions? Oh yes. Uh-huh. Uh-huh. What is my relationship with my family? And how does it "colour" my fiction. Hmmm. No, yes, no, that's interesting. Well, I'm only going to tell you this off the record, OK? Let's see. You could certainly say that the relationship has affected me. I was adopted as a small child, you see, never knew my real parents. No, no, it wasn't like that. I mean, they did their best. But it's not the same, is it? This is a theme I'm exploring at the moment in my memoirs. How the anonymousness of your parents drives you on. I'm going to call it *Sayles Patter – An Author Rings Your Bell*. Or maybe *Gary Sayles: An Extraordinary Joe*. It's all going to be in there. And that's back on the record by the way. So where were we? Right. Yes, as I said, I've got lots else I want to say. You'll thank me for it as well. It's a cut above the usual answering questions thing. It will be a real eye-opener for people who want to know what being a writer is all about. Because – no disrespect here – anyone who doesn't write can never hope to understand. I'm sorry? Oh, you are? I see. I didn't realise. Yes, that's good. Got an agent yet? Uh-huh. A friend of your father's. Of course. So what is it about, then? A 'tale of a young journalist who loses her job'? *Life Outside the Loop*? Sounds promising. And they've said what... 'Readable'? And 'High profile'? You're on the way, Miss Jones, you're on the way. That's exactly the sort of thing you'll need all right, that and scoops like the one I'm about to give you. Speaking of... once I get started I get on a roll and it's difficult to stop. So I just need to check. Are you ready for this? Are you sitting comfortably? OK. Then I'll begin. Do you remember that, by the way? *Jackanory*? I used to love that. Memory is such an important part of who we are, isn't it? Memory is like a taxi ride to your infant school... after dark. That's a phrase I'm working on at the moment. Yes, I'm experimenting with pauses. Do you remember *The Clang* – I'm sorry? Oh. Oh, OK. Well then, it happened one day as I was standing outside a bookshop. It was after one of my impromptu signing sessions, when I just pop in unannounced to see if my books are being displayed prominently enough, if they've got enough in stock, that sort of thing. There were lots of people milling about on the street. It was very busy, you know, a typical busy shopping day. And as I was standing there getting my bearings and looking at the cars and the shops and the people on the pavement, everything suddenly seemed to shrink. Everything seemed smaller, just like I was looking at them from a long way away, as though they were not real, just like they were toys. It's difficult to explain but I also seemed to have more time than anybody else, more time and more space to turn and look around. Everything was slower and less chaotic, like special effects, like really high-quality slow-motion special effects. And if that wasn't freaky enough, as I was standing there taking all of this in, I saw a bus drive past, with me on the side, a twelve-foot image of me, Gary Sayles, with my eyes looking at the street below, looking down from the side of the bus almost as if they were looking down from the sky. And then suddenly, suddenly, BANG! It all belonged to me. Everything. Just like that. Everything I could see, the shops and the cars and the people and even the stuff I couldn't see, even space and time itself – they were all mine. Every last little thing. And do you know why? It came to me then, in that moment. It's because I'm a writer, Hermione, and writers own words, and when you own words, you own everything. Everything, everything is yours, yours to be rearranged and put in place, yours to protect, yours to insure against anything harmful, yours to do anything that you want with. And so everything I could see *was* a toy, quite literally. Can you imagine? Can you picture the scene? A revelation like that on a street corner? And this revelation, I tell you it was like something special had been shown to me. Stop me if I'm getting too psychological for you here, Hermione, but I suddenly realised that all my life I'd been trying to belong. I'd been writing to say "look at me, I am one of you. I'm ordinary", when in actual fact I'm not. I've been living a lie. Kidding myself that I could be like other people. Because Gary Sayles is not and never has been an ordinary person. Gary Sayles is a writer. My first magazine piece was published when I was nineteen, my first novel when I was twenty-four. I was born a writer. And like it or not, writers are different from ordinary people, I see that now. They see more than ordinary people do. They have to. They have to balance more responsibilities than ordinary people. First to their readers. You've got to be aware of your public. Writers need readers as much as readers need writers, that's a motto of mine. But then there's yourself, you've got to do yourself justice, because it's not just about now and the relationship you have with your readers, it's not just about being accepted when you are alive, it's about later. I want to be remembered. I mean, ordinary people want to be remembered too but for a writer it's more important. That's the whole point of it, after all. And so now I realise that the People's Literature Tour is not just about carving out a niche for my work at the same time as saying thank you to my readers, it's also about saying thank you and goodbye, drawing a line under what's gone, moving on. I used to think I knew my limitations – now I realise I haven't got any. Suddenly I've got a whole new creative lease of life, suddenly I've got ambition, suddenly there's nothing I can't do, nowhere my fiction can't go. Who knows where this might lead? I don't. I can't imagine. Why not challenge myself? Maybe I'll set a novel outside of Greater London. Give my lead character different jobs. He doesn't have to be a music journalist or a lecturer in journalism: I know people in advertising as well, you know, and PR. Maybe I'll write about a man who's perfectly content to see a grey hair growing out of his nostril. Instead of writing about a man's anxiety about his masculinity, maybe I'll write from a woman's perspective, about female problems. I'm sorry? No, no, I hadn't thought of it like that, but you're getting the point, I mean I *could* do horror. Do you see, Hermione, I can do anything. I'm Gary Sayles, a writer, I own words. I'm not ordinary, I'm extraordinary and when I look down at my toys I see I can do extraordinary things. I'm Gary Sayles, after all, and *Gary Sayles can do anything, I tell you, anything at all...'*

An author gets to know
his readership

He texts her and they agree to meet at the Comfort Inn, Hyde Park. It is early in the afternoon. He is wearing a pair of Aviator shades.

As they book in he tips the receptionist a fiver and asks her 'Do you know who I am?' She says 'No,' and he says, 'I like your style, good, good,' and winks and nods his head.

In the room he sits on the bed, she paces. In her bag, the camera rolls.

'Mr Sayles. I don't know what to say. I was so nervous when I was writing that note, I had no idea whether you'd call. After all, who am I to suppose that you would want anything to do with me? You must think I'm just a giddy little star-struck fan, no better than a schoolgirl. And I suppose I am. Even so, there's something I want to ask you before we, you know, start. You've said in the past that marriage is sacred. In *Man, Woman, Baby* you described – now what was his name again? – Jake – as "a nasty piece of work" because he slept with Tiffany – the "flirty thirtysomething" – when he'd just got back from his honeymoon. I thought then that you had a low opinion of infidelity?'

'What can I say? I am a writer and writers are not bound by the same rules as normal people.'

'But your wife?'

'My wife is not like you, she does not appreciate what I am,' said Gary, and then in a voice that was pitched just a little bit higher, 'Speaking of that, no offence but do you mind if we get a bit of a wriggle on? I've got a shoot with the cable TV channel Dave this afternoon. Can't you just put your bag down and come over here? Now? Sarah?'

'Susan.'

'Whatever.' And then lower again. '*My precious.*'

And Pippa hesitates, just for a moment. And then she thinks about her art...

'Be gentle, Mr Sayles.'

'I will, my child, I will. Er, hang on a minute. Susan? What on earth is that? *Susan?* Ah. Oo. Oh. *Aa-aah.*'

An agent gets a shock

Later that afternoon, Gary rang Norwenna, bringing up her contact details on his mobile phone so quickly that he nearly dropped the slimline device in his excitement.

'Norwenna? I've got some big news! I'm going commando!' he shouted.

'I'm sorry?'

'I mean it! Like Brett Maverick! From the eponymous film! Or Bruce Willis in *Die Hard 2*! Not as violent as that obviously, but still! I'm going out on a limb!'

'Ri-ght,' said Norwenna. 'Are you OK?'

Gary, if he hadn't been on such a theme park ride of so many ecstatic twists and unexpected turns, would have spotted in her reply a certain type of hesitancy. As it was he was past caring and as his agent listened he explained to her his latest brainwave in words that flowed like a fast-flowing stream.

He told her he'd just met a fan who'd made a suggestion that would lead to the biggest revolution in publishing since the printing press or the internet. She'd told him that the great artists of days of yore had their work produced by other people. That there were internet rumours surrounding *New York Times* bestselling author James Patterson. She'd said that he, Gary Sayles, could do the same thing and hand over the writing of the rest of his London Novels (the title for the series was her idea) to other people too. Then

191

Gary would be able to branch out into new fields and avenues of fictional endeavour. Even better, these new writers didn't have to be professionals. They could be ordinary fans, chosen by a popular vote. There was a market for that sort of thing. And as his readers they'd know for sure what his readers would want to read.

It would be a win–win situation, a perfect mix of the popular Midas touch he'd made his own and the sort of business sense common only to writers who knew how to reinvent themselves, like Madonna or Lady Gaga. And even as Norwenna told him that her phone was mysteriously losing its connection, his thoughts carried on like an avalanche of excitement and he carried on shouting into a dead mouthpiece – Norwenna? *Norwenna?* – as he continued to plot the course between reclusive enigma and man of the people, between literary mogul and beacon of hope…

*In which Richard considers
one of the most difficult
questions of the whole affair*

The following morning, Richard was sitting at the till behind a pile of the collected works of one of his favourite short story writers. A handwritten sign announced 'A Tower of Babel'.

Richard was planning for London and looking again at the press release for *The Grass is Greener*. He read that 'Gary Sayles is a man who shares the values of his readers. He understands the way they feel and he isn't afraid to stand up for what they know to be right. With *The Grass is Greener*, he has once more delivered what his fans want to read: a feel-good morality tale.' And then he made a discovery.

He recognised the woman in the family portrait. The woman in the family portrait hadn't always been Mrs Gary Sayles. Her name had once been Nikki and she had worked at the Pussy Palace Sauna and Grill.

Now Richard lived for epiphanies such as this, the unexpected providing him with revelatory insights into what he was doing and why. His involvement with SNAPS had been a series of just such evolutionary lurches. But this was subtly different. This discovery drifted into his consciousness like the hit of skunkweed on an otherwise averagely destructive Saturday night, full of promise yet frightening too.

As the probable architect of the syndrome – not to mention a bloody awful writer – Gary Sayles had to be stopped. Burning his books was a good idea. It would attract the attention and capture the imagination of the liberal establishment; it might even shock the culture into accepting it had a problem. Hopefully it would also open up a discourse, and Richard knew that in any discourse, he'd have Sayles and his apologists by the theoreticals. But there was a problem with relying solely on this course of action.

Since his knock-back from the *Correspondent*, it was becoming apparent that the process would be a slow one. Not least because the medical evidence was still sketchy. So an alternative tactic – something more likely to have an immediate effect – was necessary too.

Recognising 'Nikki' suggested to Richard what this alternative might involve; the juxtaposition of 'The Author at Home with Wife Amy and Son Garfield' and the phrase 'morality tale' confirmed his instinct was on the bingo.

Sayles' Manichaean moralising was a particularly rancid element of his shtick. Richard had only just recovered from a hectoring passage on prostitution in *Cutting the Cake*. While on a stag weekend in Prague, a friend of the hero had been robbed by a sex worker he'd met in a hotel bar. The authorial tone had been revealing, the sentiment obvious: the man got a comeuppance, of sorts – in the form of a protracted argument with his 'plain' wife – but he was portrayed as an innocent abroad. The woman, by contrast, was unsympathetic and damned, arrested and sent to jail.

This, then, was the obvious course of action. Richard would contact the gutter press. The censorious and reactionary, online and in print. *Hello!* and *OK!* and the glossy lifestyle rags too; anyone, in fact, who'd consider Sayles newsworthy. He would give them a splash. An exposé of the lifestyle of a celebrity author. He would tell them that Sayles wasn't the man he made himself out to be. That even as he was planning a career out of denouncing women who worked in brothels, his wife was working in a brothel.

Richard had no doubt the tactic would work. Sayles' readers were a morally unadventurous bunch. If his outing as a hypocrite didn't faze them, mere mention of his association with the apparently black-and-white issue of prostitution surely would. The resulting outrage would put the kibosh on any post-launch sales surge of *The Grass is Greener*, and this would buy Richard and Lauren the time they needed to properly spread the word.

And yet. *And yet.* As obvious as this was, it was desperately thin stuff. Two-faced too. Richard lived to spike the non-thinking morality of the mainstream, to provoke the conservative into a more considered and progressive response to the world. In digging up a woman's past to feed their prejudices, he would instead be complicit in their vile reactionary anti-humanity. How could he justify that? To himself? To Lauren? Just what – in the name of all things dangly – was he going to do?

Richard looked again at the cover of the book. Reread the blurb, shuddered, sighed. Realised the decision had been made for him.

When the time was right, Richard would do whatever he had to do. If that involved resorting to a last resort, then so be it. He could explain his actions later. After all, nobody ever claimed that doing good by being bad was easy. For now, anything that might limit the impact of SNAPS was worth a pop. Because lives were at stake. And the time had come to shit or get off the pot...

In which Lauren speaks to the national press

Dear Ms Bevan-Jones,

I am writing to you in your capacity as critic for the *Correspondent*, with an invitation.

I am a professor of neurology at the University of Birmingham. Earlier this summer a hitherto unknown neurological condition – SNAPS – came to light. The condition results in brain death. Together with an acquaintance of mine, Mr Richard Anger (from whom I got your name), I have since accumulated a considerable volume of apocryphal trend data that points to the involvement of a certain type of novel in the development of the condition.

The novels in question are 'male confessionals'. To be specific, male confessionals written by the author Gary Sayles. Mr Sayles' latest book – *The Grass is Greener* – is due to be launched in London tomorrow and it is entirely possible that a significant number of SNAPS-related deaths will follow.

As a consequence of this, Richard and I have decided to try to bring the connection between the syndrome and Gary Sayles to the attention of the general public. Our strategy is to attend the launch and stage a ceremonial burning of *The*

Grass is Greener. And it is to this demonstration that we would like to invite you.

I attach details of the launch. If you have any questions, please do not hesitate to contact me.

Yours,
Professor Lauren Furrows

Artists for Hire.
Nothing Considered

Pippa has much film in the bag and is nearing the end of the project. She has fucked the writer and now it is time to turn her attention to the bookseller from Birmingham.

Pippa does not normally waste time on people like this, from the sadlands. They are naive, backward creatures. They are sans clue, without gorm, they lack hap. They are not from London. On this occasion, however, she is aware of her good fortune. There are these books, the man had said, that kill people. Really? she'd said. Tell me more...

She knows better, of course. Art does not kill people. No lick of paint nor photograph nor piece of music has ever caused a single death. But the bookseller and his claims have introduced another element to her film. To the destruction of Art and the ragging of the deluded. For all of his antediluvian 'more-tea-vicar?' pish, he is actually saluting the Z&P™ pennant as it regally ascends the baby-oiled blue-veined pole.

We need you to create a spectacle, he had said, make a bit of noise. Leave it to me, she'd said. I'm on it...

And she means it. There's no point in fucking people if no people are there to see it. She makes a list of het-ups and jokers. She contacts Unite Against Fascism, the English Defence League, Muslims Against

Crusades, Not Ashamed (For the Christian Foundation of our Society), UK Uncut, the Salvation Army, Outrage. She tells them that books are going to be burned, bad books by good people and good books by bad people. She calls the BBC, Sky News, ITN, some people from YouTube. She tells them that there will be a shitstorm.

Not that it is just going to be about books, of course. It is about her and Zeke too. The surface. The space beneath the surface. The Sayles project. She Facebooks 'is going to go nomnomnom with a portion of serious fun'. She tweets 'come fuck with the stars #everylast-starfucker' She corrals friendly freaks: a disco-dancing midget, a man with a monkey, a woman who eats light bulbs. She tells them there will be cameras.

And then she starts rounding up the people who'll really make the party swing.

Rhetorical question

Lauren stood on the concourse of New Street station and waited for Richard. The place echoed like a swimming pool. As she tried to listen to the announcer, she found herself going under the surface of the hubbub. Her senses dulled. Muffled sounds came to her and then disappeared as she drifted in the currents of reverie. Now there was John Clare, inside her head and clear:

Is love's bed always snow?

It was a rhetorical question. Love's bed wasn't always pristine, white. Sometimes it was less stark, more of a grey. Sometimes it changed colour, with an enticing shimmy.

Lauren thought of Richard. Even now, despite how far they'd both come, she wondered whether there was something missing between them. And yet, when it came to her experiment – when it came to how she felt about him – her interrogative impulse was weakening. Her hand had been forced by his sobriety, his efforts to change, the poem, her relaxed attitude to his advances at the art gallery. Other, less esoteric considerations had begun to make their presence felt, too. The practical arrangements of their trip to London, for one.

Standing in the waves, another line came to Lauren,

from a different poem, by a surrealist poet of her
recent acquaintance:

> 'I sleep on my feet prey to all the forms of life
> and love, and you, the only one who counts for
> me today...'

Rattling along...

Lauren glanced across the table as Richard drank from a can of McEwan's Export. 'It's the law,' he'd told her as they'd pulled out of Birmingham, 'on a train I mean,' and she'd received the news with enthusiasm. 'I'll have a gin and tonic,' she'd told him, 'for old times' sake,' and sure enough their chat had soon settled into a rhythm that she was coming to relish.

'Could you please run the arrangements past me again?' said Lauren. 'You've been a bit hazy on the details.'

'We're meeting someone down there,' said Richard.

'And who might that be?'

'She's some sort of artist, I think.'

'I see.'

'Her speciality is making a noise. There should be TV cameras and hopefully the Old Bill will get involved at some stage. All good stuff by the sounds of it. We need her too. People have got to see what we're doing, so we need someone who knows their way around the place. Someone who knows how things work down there.'

'How things work down there?'

'Yeah. London's different, you see.'

'And why might that be?'

'It's full of mountebanks and shitheads, for a start.'

'How very pleasant.'

'Why, thank you.'

'You're welcome.'

Lauren drummed her fingers on the table, sipped her G&T. She told Richard that she had contacted the *Correspondent*, filled them in on her latest clinical research. Then she checked her watch – was that all it was? – and tried to slow down the connections that were firing so spectacularly in her brain. She turned her attention to the world outside the window. Tried to focus on the flat countryside, on blurred snapshots of dull towns. They passed through Long Buckley, Wolverton, Bletchley. It was no good. They were in-between names, transitional places. What fun a mediocre writer could have with the metaphorical implications of such an environment!

'I get the impression she's one of these ironic types,' she heard Richard say, and was minded to continue the ritual to-fro.

'I thought you didn't "do" irony? I thought you said irony was a "cop-out"?'

'Only when it becomes the message. When it's trowelled on without finesse by people piling irony on irony, taking all substance out of the equation. What do they want us to do? Engage with shadows?'

'Ah yes, but isn't life about that in many respects? Engaging with the indefinable? With what has gone and what might be? It's not all about the here and now.'

'Yes, but something has to have been there in the first place. Words, just words, aren't enough, however smart or pretty they are. Smart and pretty with nothing beneath is just as mediocre as dumb and generic.'

'But I thought you said smart was good?'

'Typical you. Analytical to the last. Smartarse, then. It's a fine distinction. And do you know what? Today, Lauren, I'm the man to make it.'

Lauren raised her eyebrows, theatrically and without compunction. When she was with him, she was somehow more aware of her body. Of what it could do. Of its possibilities. As they pulled into Beaconsfield she felt herself flush. She hoped it was from the gin.

'Would you like another drink?' she asked.

'Are you having one?' replied Richard and then, before she answered, he added, 'Nah, don't think I'll bother,' and this felt right too. She was giddy enough as it was and London was looming.

The train eased away from the platform and Richard saw Lauren's eyes flitting self-consciously around his face. He flashed her his patented bad man's grin, tried to relax into it, couldn't.

'So what do you reckon, then?' said Richard. 'How do you think we're doing?'

'I think it's going to be a struggle,' said Lauren. 'I really am rather afraid of how it might all turn out.'

'I think you're right to be. I mean, I sometimes wonder what I'm going to do next, so what chance have you got?'

'Very droll,' said Lauren. 'But I think you protest too much. I think you're quite focused on a happy ending.'

'Please don't say that. I don't believe in happy endings.'

'Why ever not?'

'Well, they're such a cliché, aren't they? And who likes a cliché?'

But the joviality was now forced. As the next station came and went and then the next, they both became quiet and the happy rattle of their conversation was replaced by the other sounds of the train as they got closer to London and to the books that killed.

In which Zeke approves
of James May

Zeke is getting ready to meet Gary Sayles. He has read most of *The Grass is Greener*. It has been like eating Jaffa Cakes.

Zeke's disguise is growing more convincing by the day. He has been ringing up the traffic people on Radio 2, with news of localised delays. He has booked himself into a gym. He has started to watch *Top Gear*. He has changed his mobile phone to get a better deal and downloaded a new ringtone. It is Katy Melua's instant classic from the noughties, 'Closest Thing to Crazy'.

He likes the feeling the book has given him. It is almost as though he has tapped into a former life that he didn't know he'd had. From a time when things were simpler.

Mike meets Gary Sayles outside the church in Bloomsbury. There are columns, a tiered tower that looks like the wedding cake on the cover illustration from the author's collected works. Gary greets him as he would an old acquaintance who has fallen on bad times. They go inside.

The church is decorated down either side of the nave with eight six-foot-high posters of Gary Sayles' face. They have red borders. In some he is thoughtful, staring into the middle distance, his fist to his chin. In some he is looking down and laughing at a private joke. There is a small stage and a microphone stand where the pulpit should be. Hanging behind the stage is a backdrop bearing the legend 'The People's Literature Tour'. The words are laid over a bright yellow sun. Mike feels the hairs standing up on the back of his neck.

'What do you think?' says Gary.

'I don't know what to say.'

'I didn't want to go over the top,' says Gary, 'I just need to let these people know that in these difficult times they can turn to me for guidance. Because that is what I offer. Something important. Something more important than pop music or television or even film.'

Patsies

In a pub around the corner from the church, Pippa meets the bookseller from the boondocks and his doris. Pippa has ingested half a gram of sweaty base, a line of posh and half a little fella to take the edge off. She is in control. The bookseller is wide-eyed and sweaty. Worn by a Sue Ryder suit. He is inhaling a Guinness. The woman looks as though she would be very pretty if only she'd take her glasses off. Except she isn't wearing glasses. She is drinking Bombay Sapphire and tonic. Pippa wonders why she is here. She looks at people with interest and when they look back she turns away. She is not well practised at life. There is something between her and the bookseller, almost like sexual energy. It is coincidence maybe, or bad timing.

Anger says to Pippa, 'So is it all ready? Have you got everything ready? We've sorted out the books. I hope everything's all right at your end.'

'Yeah, everything's ready. You said you wanted to make some noise? I've organised some noise all right. There's two terrestrial, a broadsheet, a red-top, a satellite, some cable and three glossies on stream. The usual denizens of the social media scene. You won't know what's hit you. Just make sure you've got your part sorted out.'

'Oh, we're just here to fan the flames,' says Anger.

'Quite literally,' says the woman.

They both try to laugh, but they are not looking cool. They are looking jittery, as though their fantasy is taking its toll. The woman glances at Pippa, on the sly. Anger picks at the shoulders of his whistle. Puts his hand in his trouser pocket, dresses from the right to the left and back again.

'Remember,' he says, 'we're not the bad guys here. We aren't burning the books because of what they say, but because they say nothing.'

This is too easy, thinks Pippa. They are close to the end now. Everything is in place. Zeke has surpassed himself. He has immersed himself in the Method. She knows she can rely on Gary Sayles. Which leaves this Angry sort and his Little Miss Nothing Eyes. Fools they may be, but turbo-keen too. And her film means nothing without the enthusiasm of fools.

Pippa laughs.

It is good that they are all here.

For her.

For Zeke.

For their triumph.

A film

It is later. Pippa is filming. It is a good turn-out. A freak show, a riot, a circus. A cacophonous mass gathers in front of the church. The air is violent with screams, whistles, bagpipes. The crowd has stopped the traffic on the Euston Road. At the edges of the scrum the press roves, with booms, in frowning bunches. There are three television camera crews. What's it all about?

The bookseller is burning the books in a brazier in front of the church. The books burn quickly. The flames are red and yellow, orange, blue and brown. Two fire engines are parked on the road. Their crews are agitated, togged up, waiting on the word. The crowd is stopping them from reaching the flames. Overhead a chopper circles; on the ground Police Support Units have overtime on their mind.

The throng is impolite. Over to one side, the EDL and Muslims Against Crusades are involved in a stand-off. A copy of *Mein Kampf* is set alight then thrown into the air, followed by a Koran. A white van turns up, *Dave's Meats* on the side. Within minutes, the air is thick with pork tenderloin. Two members of Outrage have hung a banner between the columns of the church. It says *Perverts Undermining State Scrutiny*. Now they are showering the crowd with Boys Own condoms. This seems to inflame the evangelical Not Ashamed, who have been waiting for some time to be offended. They respond by reciting the Lord's Prayer through loudhailers. The Sally Army contingent bangs tambourines and tries to minister to a George Clinton tribute band whom they've mistaken for the homeless; their uniforms cause similar confusion among the hitherto angrily unfocused Unite Against Fascism. Ugliness ensues.

There is more. Pippa skirts the fringes of the melee and has a spin around the car park at the back of the church. A mariachi band strikes up as a troupe of burlesque dancers start to remove items of clothing. 'Where do you want us, Pip?' asks a man in a Babygro, 'and where's all the photographers?'

And then, at the front of the building, at the centre of it all, she focuses on a queue of people, buttressed by coppers, winding through crash barriers like a gut. They are waiting to get inside the church. They are smart casuals. They are wearing Cotton Traders, Timberland, Rockport. Pippa looks at the faces of the people in the queue. Some are anxious. Some alarmed. Most bemused.

We need to shock them out of their complacency! the bookseller had said. But the people in the queue are clearly not to be shocked, not by any of it. And certainly not by burning books. Pippa knows that they have a more straightforward relationship with the world than this. They are consumers. They know what they like and they like Gary Sayles. They are not concerned with the context in which his books appear. Why would they be? All they are interested in is the three hundred pages of their next moralistic nod-in.

It is a motif moment.

The people in the queue will make the final cut.

Richard fails again

Richard shrugged off the attentions of a Hassidic Jew in a shtreimel and a tutu and threw another book on to the fire. He was hoarse but still he hollered:

'MEDIOCRITY KILLS! SAY NO TO MEDIOCRITY! PROTECT YOUR MIND!'

and as he ran out of energy:

'DON'T READ SHIT AND DIE! READ FOR YOUR LIVES!'

It was no good. But then he'd clocked that from the off. As soon as he'd started shouting, Lauren had disappeared into the melee and without her there Richard had been overcome by the familiar feeling of pissing into the wind.

He'd blamed the artist, at first, for the debacle. What she thought she was doing was beyond him. Sure, she'd provided a fire. And he'd seen some flyers decorated with the face of Gary Sayles and the word '*murderer!*' But there was also a monkey in a studded leather collar. A stilt-walker in a kilt. An old dear in a latex nun's outfit. Some twat in a gas mask. Not to mention johnnies, everywhere johnnies.

But it wasn't her fault, not really. He hadn't been clear enough about what he wanted. And even though the spectacle had been empty, it was undoubtedly spectacular.

It was the response of the people in the queue that had been most disappointing. They were here for Sayles, of course, but even so. Half an hour he'd been standing there, hollering and beckoning like a nutter and barker, spittling love and vitriol and reason. The least they could have done was come over to him, ask him what he was shouting about or why he was burning the books. Then he could have opened their minds. Explained about the perils of mediocrity, talked them back from the brink. Yet no one seemed to care.

It didn't matter that he'd always been on their side. Given them the benefit of the doubt. *Give people the choice*, he'd always said, *give them the choice* and they'd wake up, discover new ways to engage with the world, new ways to entertain themselves. Even new ways to switch off, if that was what they wanted. Here they were. Hunkering down. Uninterested, passive, supine. Walking right past him and into the arms of Sayles with not so much as a pause to think about the implications of the flames.

It was obviously too late. The bromidic deluge had clearly been too much to withstand, too relentless. They were too far gone, not drowning in a sea of mediocrity but splashing contentedly about, wasting that little bit more of evolution with the passing of every non-discerning day, rejoicing by default in flat lives that led only to dull affairs and more of the same...

And yet. And yet. If the demonstration hadn't provoked the necessary response, if it hadn't stimulated a desire for something different or a need for something more, this wasn't necessarily the fault of either the artist or the people in the queue. Not for the first time that summer, a more devastating conclusion was possible: it was Richard himself who had failed.

He sighed, an exhalation that ended in a roar, tossed the last copy of *The Grass is Greener* into the flames. Then he saw him. Stepping out of a white stretch limo as it pulled up behind a cordon of baton-wielding Old Bill. Gary Sayles. The man himself, in all his obscene glory, not ten short metres away. As the author stood there, with his hands on his hips, Richard could see his brain chugging. A flunkey passed him a flyer. He read it, raised his chin. Looked confused, then vexed.

At the sight of his would-be nemesis, Richard was newly invigorated, newly enraged. This was his moment. He would make an impression here tonight if he had to punch a bestselling idiot to do it. He began to fight his way through the crowd. Progress was slow. Someone got in his face, speaking in tongues, and he told them to fuck off. He slipped on a smear of monkey shit, nearly went down. 'Get out of my way!' he bellowed, as he drop-kicked a transvestite dwarf. 'Do you hear me? I'm warning you!' He was closer now, saw Sayles duck a low-flying mini pork pie. 'I'll give you a contentious trip to IKEA!' he continued. 'Up yer authorly arse!' and then he was suddenly within reach, close enough to the author to hear him ambushed by a journalist and to hear his consternation – 'mediocrity? What do they know of mediocrity? Have they sold words? *HAVE THEY SOLD WORLDS?*' – close enough to hurl a futile 'Oi!' before the shitsucker was wrapped up by security men and led away in the direction of the church.

It was then that Richard was hit by the first blast of water from the firefighter's hose.

The People's Literature Tour

Pippa edges her way along the queue of people still filing into the church. The people are dusted with ash. She sees Richard blasted by a hose, fall back into a camera crew, his woman emerge from the crowd. As if on cue a siren sounds and then Pippa is past the doormen and inside the church.

Inside, the crowd is anxious for the main event. Pippa films twitching heads, fidgeting eyes. The church is full. The lights are up. The decor is really bad. The place is decked out with jejune, schoolboy iconography.

Pippa asks a couple, 'What do you think about what's going on out there?' and the man replies, 'What's it all about? Who are those people?' and the woman says, 'We've only come along to buy the book,' and the man says, 'That's right. It's so true to life, what he writes. He could be writing about us.'

Then the church is hushed and the lights dim and the din from outside has quieted and Pippa turns to film Gary Sayles, who has appeared on stage.

'Ladies and gentlemen,' says Gary, 'my name is Gary Sayles and I'd like to thank you all for coming here tonight. I'll keep it short. Tonight is not about the pathetic animals outside, whoever they are, whatever they're trying to prove. It is not about their ridiculous claims about my work. It is not about their antisocial violence and vandalism. It is about my writing and what it means to you and the hundreds of thousands of people like you up and down the country who read my books every day.

'It's a way of saying "come with me and I will show you the way", a way of saying "together we can achieve" and a way of saying "watch this space".

'Ladies and gentlemen, I give you *The Grass is Greener*.

'I give you the people and the literature, the literature for the people.

'I give you the People's Literature Tour!'

There is much applause. The clapping is an infectious release. People are clapping because people next to them are clapping. They are on safe ground again. Then Gary disappears and Zeke is up on stage. He looks dedicated. Pippa is running out of film, but Zeke has started and Pippa knows it is all over bar the reading, there is only the reading to go.

Lauren gets on with it

Richard stood outside the church and shivered in the flashing lights of the emergency services. The ground was covered in soggy strings of flyer and ash. Juggling balls were sudsy in pools of spume. The PUSSY banner had come free from one of its moorings and on the other side of the road a flag of St George was wrapped around a lamp-post, desultory and pointless. There were condoms. Of course there were condoms.

A posse of flash mobbers stood around sending each other photos, but nearly everyone else had left the scene. Most of the protesters had made off or been kettled in the car park; only UK Uncut remained, angered at Gary Sayles' apparent offshore investments, sitting proudly defiant in a circle.

Richard was wet through. His suit hung off him like a badly fitting personality. He thought back to 'The Author at Home with Wife Amy and Son Garfield'.

So this was how his great crusade ended. The noble anti-hero reduced to a shoddy gesture of bitter resignation, to flicking peanuts at the suit at the end of the bar. Grinding his molars, he reached for his phone. Tomorrow he would resort to his last resort. Manufacture a 'scandal' where none existed. And if he was going to piss on the poor woman's cornflakes, the least he could do was give her a heads-up.

He made the call. Stared at his shoes. Then he felt

a hand in the small of his back. It was Lauren. Blimey. He'd almost forgotten about Lauren...

'Richard?'

'Where the hell have you been?'

'Watching. It's a good turn-out, isn't it? What about you?'

'Getting wet. Getting really wet.'

'I saw that!'

'And distraught. Really wet and really distraught.'

'Oh. Why?'

'Didn't you see their reaction? We've been wasting our time. They're the walking dead.'

'Not necessarily. Don't forget, these are his diehard fans. And I've spoken to a lot of the press tonight. There's still a chance that word will get out before the epidemic takes hold.'

'Perhaps. But there's something else. The other day, you asked me if I'd changed. Well, of course I have. You've changed me. But tonight I needed to show I still had it in me, that I could still get to people, antagonise them, wind them up. That I could still provoke them, still be bad. Well, I can't. I don't know if I ever could. I'm not actually that good at being bad, you see, just as I'm not that bad at being good. And you know what that means, don't you?'

'I do. It means you're just like the rest of us. Reduced to moving ourselves forward, incrementally, day by day. Well, poor you.'

Lauren shook her head. She'd seen enough. They'd talked enough. She felt enough. Her experiment was drawing to a close, and at least one of its conclusions was already apparent. She was ready.

'Anyway,' she said, 'this is no time for self-indulgence. It might interest you to know that while you've been wallowing, I've had another idea. About what we can do about SNAPS. We're not finished yet, not by a long way.'

'Really? What do you have in mind?'

'I'll tell you tomorrow. We can sort the details out over breakfast.'

'Tomorrow? *Over breakfast?*'

'Yes. You didn't think we were going home, did you?'

'Oh. *What?* You mean... you don't mean... do you?'

'Oh, for goodness' sake Richard, you're not making this easy. Do I have to spell it out?'

And as she headed into the church, Lauren felt a great and liberating rush of what she could only describe as relief.

'Yes,' she called over her shoulder, 'yes, I do mean...'

A new life begins

Gary Sayles left the church by the side entrance. He raised his hand presidentially to a riot policeman. He had seen enough. The little people had turned out in force and were putty in his hands and, like putty, he could mould them into anything he wanted, like statues or models of Jabba the Hutt from Part Three of the original *Star Wars* trilogy. There was no alternative, no escape for any of them. And Gary Sayles?

Gary Sayles was on Cloud Ten. His life was building to a climax. Tonight, he was leaving these people behind. To their old certainties. He would continue to produce books for them, of course, one way or another, but he himself was changing horses in midstream, moving through the gears to a new set of conventions. From now on, he was going to live his life by a different set of rules.

He had started by cutting the apron strings. It had been a brave move leaving his audience in the church to their own devices, while they still wanted more of his presence. It felt funny too: Gary used to revel in mingling with his public. But he'd realised that the People's Literature Tour wasn't just about giving his readers a fair crack of the promotional whip, it was also about managing their expectations. He'd made the introductions tonight because it was the first night of the tour, but there came a point in every successful writer's life when it made commercial sense to distance yourself from your readers. The farther removed you were, the greater the air of mystery – and hence anticipation – that surrounded your actions. Did *New York Times* bestselling author James Patterson still press the flesh of his fans? Gary thought it unlikely.

Gary reached Euston Square station. He had planned to take the tube home, one last time, for old times' sake. He'd a new book out, after all.

But something was telling him not to. Something was telling him to make a clean break.

Gary listened to the voice. He dialled a cab on his phone. When it arrived he sat in the back and felt he was looking down on the city once more, as if from the sky.

A few streets from his home, he asked the driver whether he could be dropped off. He was. He walked unhurriedly, his hands in his bespoke trouser pockets. As he crossed Notting Hill Gate, Gary saw his image on a billboard, the first of many that would appear over the next few weeks. Gary was part of the landscape of this city. There were a thousand billboards in the city and each of them told a thousand stories. But none of them was quite as unique as his.

He was everywhere. This was his world. Everyone else was just visiting.

And how!

SNAPS

Pippa's camera is still rolling. The crowd are polite. Zeke is coming to the end of his reading. He is stumbling over the odd word now. The odd list. 'Ten reasons not to have a one-night stand' takes two minutes. He looks tired. He has done well. It has been an effort.

Pippa does one last sweep around the church. Sweet JellyBaby-Jeebus she has some material here. The tracking shot pans back to the stage just in time to catch Zeke crumpling to the ground, and as she sees the life leave his body, the camera records her scream, a terrible sound, timeless and unknowing...

At the back of the church, Lauren shuddered as the crowd noise rose in yelps and whimpers. She stood her ground as the mass of people eddied and flowed in distressed confusion, saw the woman she'd come to find.

'Hermione Bevan-Jones? I'm Lauren Furrows.'

'What's happening? What's going on?' asked Hermione.

And Lauren said:

'It's started...'

The Pussy Palace
Sauna and Grill

Later that evening, Amy listened to Richard's message. It was difficult to hear, but it demanded her full attention.

'Hello? *Hello?* This is a message for Nikki. Or Amy Sayles, whichever you like. I'm just phoning to tell you that I know who you are. I mean who you were. What you were. At the Pussy Palace. Now you have to know that this doesn't bother me, not in the slightest, I mean, I'm really not being judgemental here. But your husband, well, he's a bad man and he needs to be stopped. And it looks like the only way I can get to him is through you. So. All I can say is it might be an idea if you stayed away from the papers for a while. I'm going to have to tell them what you used to do, you see. To get at him. It's the only way. The last resort. Believe me, if there was another way, I'd... Shit. I'm running out of cred...'

SNAPS

The next day *The Grass is Greener* began its terrible
work. In all major cities and towns across the UK
people died suddenly and seemingly without reason.
Lives ended on streets, on buses, in offices and trains
and homes.

Large gatherings of people reported multiple deaths.
By midday several halls of the NEC in Birmingham
were cordoned off following an incident in which
four delegates to the 5th Annual Symposium on
Travel and Tourism failed to emerge after a break
for soft drinks and assorted cream-filled biscuits.
Visitors to a Financial Services Exhibition in Harrogate
were decimated. Other concentrations of loss of life
included Windsor, Sutton Coldfield and Luton, while
at book distribution centres in Norwich, Colchester
and Eastbourne, the toll was two dozen before the
morning was out.

By the end of lunchtime, London was hot with
fear and feverish with news and speculation. Radio
and television carried coverage of the sudden deaths.
There was panic and talk of panic. Sirens sounded,
people ran. At Number Ten, a war room was set
up, a session of COBRA convened. NBC suits were
issued to armed police and then recalled. Six deaths
in the offices of the Highways Agency, Buckingham
Palace Road, resulted in the royal residence being
sealed off with tanks and armoured vehicles. The

infrastructure of the city buckled in the violence of the alarm. Traffic stopped, cars were abandoned. On the 12.05 from Bank to St Paul's, a man read over another's shoulder and paid the ultimate price; within an hour, the number of deaths on the underground led to the closure of the entire network. At Heathrow airport, flights were grounded after several minutes of carnage amongst browsers in Terminals One, Two and Four, where *The Grass is Greener* was being promoted as part of a Buy One Get One Free campaign in WH Smith.

At one o'clock in the afternoon the prime minister, Home Secretary and Commissioner of the Metropolitan Police Force appeared at a news conference at Number Ten and appealed for calm. They were close to identifying the cause of the deaths, they said, and steps were being taken to prevent more. Their words were not reassuring. No one knew which way to turn, at whom or what to point the finger or where to direct the relevant authorities. By then the nationwide death toll stood at more than four hundred. Two hundred and fifty had died in the capital alone. And still there was no definitive connection between the books and the dead; no one knew what was striking the people down.

Later, human interest tales emerged from under the pale sheets of death, thick-blooded with poignancy. In the Piccadilly branch of the largest retail book chain three goods-in staff, the fiction buyer and a publishing rep dropped dead before the title even hit the sales floor. Particularly resonant was the loss of life on the Tottenham Court Road, in the canteen of a satellite office of the accountants to Barker Follinge. There, a carelessly discarded copy of *The Grass is Greener* killed seven inquisitive employees, one after the other, the bodies lying where they fell.

In which Lauren backs a hunch and Richard is prepared to compromise

Earlier that morning, Lauren and Richard had finished their breakfast and gone back up to their room. They had allowed themselves some downtime, but now it was time to get to work. They switched on the news channel, propped themselves up on the bed and opened Lauren's iPad.

'Right,' said Lauren. 'So there's a few mentions here and there, but I think we should accept the fact that the coverage of last night isn't on the scale – or of the tone – that we had hoped for. So we need to settle on a more immediate course of action. Do you have any suggestions?'

Richard thought about 'Nikki', said, 'No.'

'OK. Well, I've been working on an alternative hypothesis that may indicate a way forward. It goes back to the pathology of the syndrome. In the case of the first death – the editor Elizabeth Menzies, in the taverna on Corfu – although she was technically "reading" a Sayles book when she collapsed, there was no evidence that she was actually turning the pages at the precise time of her death. This means that, despite its acronym, SNAPS may not always occur spontaneously. In some cases it will; but in some it might actually be a delayed reaction. Are you with me?'

'Yes, of course I am. It's not rocket science, is it? And I mean that literally. It's neurology and cultural criticism and a little bit of guesswork and...'

'Richard? I know you're excited. But we need to get this right. Can you concentrate? So. Bringing us back to today, this opens up the possibility that we may have time to alter the neural networking of people who will have encountered the book, but are still alive. In theory, allowing us the opportunity to introduce a factor that will recharge the electrical impulses in their brain cells, thus preventing the atrophy from reaching a fatal level. Now logically speaking, anything could perform this function: a TV programme, a film, a piece of music, a conversation. But as you keep telling me, books are different. And as it is only books that are powerful enough to trigger the onset of the syndrome, we have to work on the assumption that it is only books that can arrest and reverse it. Do you see?'

'I do.'

'Good. Because I've had an idea. It's a big one too, and daft, almost big and daft enough to be one of yours. And if it's going to work I need your help. I need you to think carefully, to select a number of authors, maybe half a dozen. Writers who hit people over the head, but not too hard. They must be intelligent but not too obviously highbrow, literary but not too dense. And they must make you... what was it you said? Dribble and ogle and snort? Hmm. Maybe not quite that. We can't afford to put people off, they can't be too "out there". How about if we just say they have to alter your perceptions, shift your perspective. Make you feel or think differently about life? Or even better, as it's mediocrity that's got us here, how about if they're just good? You know. Verifiably good? Do you understand?'

'Got you,' said Richard.

And he began to make a list.

In which Lauren takes charge and Richard continues his parlay with the mainstream

At midday, Lauren, Richard and Hermione Bevan-Jones arrived at the offices of the *Correspondent*. Hermione knocked on her father's door.

'Daddy?'

'Monie. Come in, please.'

'Daddy, do you remember taking a phone call about a week ago? About that new Gary Sayles book, *The Grass is Greener*?'

'Vaguely. Dreadful Scouse fellow, banging on about bad eggs in the commercial fiction barrel. Sounded like he'd been at the poteen. What of it?'

'Well, have you seen any news today? There's been a number of unexplained deaths, all over the city. And I think this might have something to do with it.'

'Oh, Monie. Do you honestly believe...'

'Mr Bevan,' said Lauren, 'we don't have time for this,' and Alistair Bevan recognised the third storey in her voice and kept quiet as she continued.

'My name is Lauren Furrows. I'm a professor of neurology at the University of Birmingham. I need to tell you that we are facing a public health disaster, that we are in a position to limit its effects and that we need the help of a newspaper such as the *Correspondent* to do so. Firstly I would ask that you post the following statement on the news and books pages of your website. Secondly, I assume that someone on the paper has contacts within the Cabinet Office? Because we need to meet with someone in a position of power, and soon. Please be good enough to speak to whoever and arrange this meeting. Oh, and I forgot to mention. Accompanying me will be my colleague, Richard Anger. He's something of an authority on the situation.'

Blimey! It's Bertolt Brecht!

It is the afternoon. Zeke is dead. Pippa has not slept for thirty-six hours. Zeke is dead. Pippa has not grieved. There are some things she cannot face. She is consumed instead with thoughts of revenge. With the need to create an enduring work of art, a piece of work that illustrates that all paint and ink and film and music has an effect. That all art means something. Not just anything consumers want it to mean. But stuff.

It has been a long day and a half. Pippa has been googling assiduously. She has memorised John Keats' hymn to the written word, 'On First Looking into Chapman's Homer'. She has read up on Harriet Shaw Weaver, whose devotion to what she considered 'important' writing enabled the experimental modernism of James Joyce to reach a sceptical world. She has digested the Stuckist manifestos. They concern Art. Point 9 of 'Remodernism' says: '*Spiritual art is not about fairyland.* It is about taking hold of the rough texture of life. It is about addressing the shadow and making friends with wild dogs. Spirituality is the awareness that everything in life is for a higher purpose.' Point 8 of 'Anti-Anti-Art' says: 'Conceptualism is so called not because it generates a plethora of concepts, but because it never manages to progress beyond one single concept, namely Duchamp's original thought.'

Now she is ready.

She begins her work of art. It is a high-concept piece. Even witty. Pippa is pre-post-ironic. As she considers the details, she is wearing a flat cap, a pair of dungarees and a pair of clogs.

She perfects an invisible ink solution out of Mackeson stout and borax. She uses this solution to write slogans on two blank business cards. One says: 'Art is not a mirror held up to reality. Art is a hammer with which to shape the world.' The other says: 'Boy meets girl. So what.' They are from the politically charged playwright Bertolt Brecht. They will form part of her work.

Pippa draws (crude) diagrams of pulleys and weights. She calculates the velocity of swinging objects, weighs suitable books. Guesses the height of Gary Sayles, tests the strength of fishing line. Looks at the physiology of the skull, reads up about knots and catches and hooks. It is a process that takes pains. Pippa has been meticulous with her calculations. But she has worked quickly.

On the streets outside there is terror. Inside her head is madness. The hours of last night passed naked and screaming. In the early morning she rang the author and left a message on his mobile. By now he will be on his way to the Comfort Inn for another rendezvous with his besotted fan. She will go to his house. And set up her work of art.

A woman scorned

Later that morning Amy found the book on the bed in the spare room. Gary had recently taken to sleeping in there. The book was A3, bound in red leather. He had left it out for her to see. He needed his stories to be seen.

On the title page Gary had written 'My Diary' and then he'd crossed out the 'My' and put 'A' and then he'd crossed out the 'Diary' and written 'Journal'.

On the next page Amy read:

'Susan, oh Susan, oh Susan. Oh Susan Susan Susan. Susan oh Susan Susan Susan Susan Susan, Suzie Suze Susan Sue.

'Today is the first day of the rest of my life. Today I have taken a mistress and a muse and, like a simple man who has tasted the finest caviar or dark turkey meat at the family Christmas meal for the first time, I have been given a taste of the way I shall live.'

Amy didn't turn to the next page. She had shed her tears. Last night and in the nights before that. Tears of frustration and anger. Amy knew that she and Garfield – 'the firstborn' – had not been a part of Gary's fiction for some time. Now it was time to use her imagination, to take control. To write her husband out of her life. To begin a new story with her son.

Who had made the phone call the previous night? Amy didn't know or care. The whole situation was bitter with hypocrisy. It reminded her of what she knew lay behind most everyday tales of Man and Woman. But whatever else he had said, the man's information had been accurate. Amy had been Nikki, seven years and several narratives ago, at the Pussy Palace Sauna and Grill. And the call had given her an idea.

So the caller was going to 'expose' her as a former sex worker? Fine. She would use this farcical state of affairs to her advantage. To show Gary what happened when he tried to write her out of his life.

Not that she would allow the man on the end of the phone to fuck her husband up. That was something she would do herself.

An imaginative hypothesis

Amy packed a suitcase, bought herself and Garfield train tickets. She upturned furniture and opened drawers in her kitchen, sent an email to the local police station. Disguised herself in dark glasses and took her boy with her to catch a train to somewhere far away...

Artist at work

Fifteen minutes later, Pippa breaks in round the back of the Sayles house and begins to install her artwork.

Consciousness and the Novel

For all of his omnipotence and power as a greater mortal, Gary Sayles was never aware of his role in the death that swept across the UK. Similarly, he would have no idea that in the afternoon of that murderous day his wife had sent an email to Notting Hill police station, expressing concern over his potentially violent reaction to forthcoming revelations about her past – 'He has a vicious temper. I fear for my life.' Nor that the same station had then received an anonymous phone call – again from Amy but supposedly from concerned passers-by – about a screaming argument between the author and his wife, that could be heard from the street outside his house. Nor that he would – under less extraordinary circumstances – be a suspect in an assault on Amy and implicated in the subsequent disappearance of his wife and child...

For Pippa had worked well. Early that evening Gary returned from his would-be get-together with Susan. When she had called him overnight and suggested they meet again, she'd told him she might be late and to wait for her. She had sounded distant and although he hadn't seen her there, Gary knew that she would have been overwhelmed by the launch of *The Grass is Greener*. But Susan had not arrived.

Gary stayed at the Comfort Inn from two until three o'clock and then set off home. After he had been forced to wait an inordinate length of time for a cab, he realised that dark and alien forces were at play in his city. He quickly forgot his disappointment in his tardy muse and, stopping only to buy a velvet waistcoat on the way, he hurried back to Notting Hill on foot. He had work to do. Writing. In this uncertain time, people would need reassurance that everything was right with the world. That there was nothing to worry about. People would need Gary Sayles.

He arrived home at around five o'clock. He opened his front door and stepped into his porch. Flicked a light switch. Checked for another key in his waistcoat pocket. Opened the inside door.

As he moved into the wide hallway of his home he just had time to blink before he walked into Pippa's work of art and his head was caught between two hardback books – suspended from the ceiling and connected to the inside front door by a series of catches and loops – that swung in deadly arcs, a copy of *The History of Roget's Thesaurus* and *Consciousness and the Novel* by David Lodge, two heavy hardback books which split and crushed his skull, which squashed his head and squeezed his pureed brains up and out through splintering bone and flecked and splashed them bloody and grey on to the walls and the ceiling and the covers of the books as they hung there swinging and his body fell to the floor.

Books

Early the following morning it rained books. The previous evening there had been announcements from all broadcast media outlets. Anyone who'd read any of *The Grass is Greener* – or had spoken to someone who had – was to go home and sit in a darkened room until the books landed. They were then to make their way to the emergency drop sites, in silence, pick up a novel and start reading. Sleep was recommended while they were waiting for the arrival of the RAF and at the end of the announcement all radio, television and internet signals were blocked. Just to be on the safe side...

And so it was that Jim Crace fell from the sky. Alison Moore and Henry Sutton and Hilary Mantel fell from the sky, Ali Smith and Marcus Mills too. Their books fell from the sky in their thousands, parachuted into parks and on to roundabouts in towns and cities across the barren and would-be suburban land. The heavens opened and the sky streamed ink; it poured with hope and despair, speculation and horror, it pissed down passion, intelligence and love. Wisdom fell from the sky, acuity fell from the sky, generosity and experimentation fell from the sky, in voices as clear as life-giving water – now satiric, now declarative, now saint-like, now sick – voices that were no longer muffled by the darkness of commercial neglect or drowned out by a babble of low-level discourse and the lackaday observations of insensate cultural goons; lives fell from the sky, in whole lives or fragments, half-lives and double lives, hidden lives made tangible by plain speaking and made-up words, by prose that was spare or fantastic, rambunctious, filthy, alien, poetic or untrue; these were lives brought to life by the curiosity and hard work of magicians and scientists for whom the world and its infinities was to be monkeyed with or pored over, fissured for the wonder of the process, spat on, believed in or merely rewired for kicks.

And brains absorbed the books and drank them thirstily in as they got back to work, becoming fertile again, and nourished by the ideas and emotions, the voices and creations, the quiet purpose and hollered violence of the striven-for art, by the words that ran into words and then on, in drops and droplets and torrents that re-fizzed connections and washed energy and sentience into matter with their vital precision or the life-giving force of their flow.

And books did what they were supposed to do.

Lauren and Richard

It was a month later. They sat on a bench in the park. The sky was grey and brown. It was November and they sat close to each other in the cold. They looked at the trees away across the park. There were short trees, thick trunked and menacing. There were trees that were tall and thin against the city sky. They were elegant, the foliage tapered like buds. The two of them sat for some time without speaking.

'It's nice this,' said Lauren, 'isn't it?'

'It is,' said Richard, 'it is.'

The past six months had been good to Lauren. She had felt the breath of passion in her life and she had welcomed it, even though it had sometimes been from the morning after the night before. She had wrestled with her past and subdued it and taken it with her into the dark; only occasionally had it bitten her on the arse. She had been introduced to a friendship that had been confusing and imperfect and true. And, of course, she had taken a lover.

And for Richard? A peace, of sorts, at last? Well, what do you think?